A TICKET TO MURDER

Abby L. Vandiver

ISBN: 979-88428549-1-2

Media Web Publishing

Cover Design by Shondra C. Longino

Chapter One

"Chi é?" I said.

"Who is it?" was one of the phrases I'd learned in my *Complete Italian* book before I'd taken my rebound trip to Italy. The book was not only supposed to teach me Italian but also how to communicate in real-life situations in Italy. Unfortunately, it had said nothing about what to do when a stranger came a-knocking at six o'clock in the morning.

I stood pushing the weight of my five-foot-four, one hundred twenty-pound body against the door, bracing myself in case the person on the other side tried to ram it open. I waited for an answer.

"*Ho un messaggio per* Rowan Bell," the early morning strangler—uh I meant stranger promptly replied.

I'd heard "*messaggio*." I was almost sure that was the word for message. And Rowan Bell was me. He at least wasn't trying to act as if he'd mistakenly knocked on the wrong door. I put the safety latch on and pulled the door open enough to peer out with one eye.

I recognized the uniform. It was the bell hop from the hotel.

"*Si?*" I said.

He stuck out his hand. "*Per te,*" he said.

"For me?" I answered back in English.

"*Si,*" he said, nodding, a smile across his face too pleasant for such an early hour.

He had a brown envelope. I could see my name clearly written across the front. And there was a postmark with a stamp that didn't look familiar.

Who would send something to my hotel room? I thought. I looked down at his hand and back up at him. Who knew I was even staying here? I turned and looked back into the room. I saw my cell phone sitting on the nightstand where I had left it the night before. I was sure by now it was fully charged—no reason for any missed messages or calls.

I took in a breath as thoughts of possible dangers ran through my mind. This wasn't the 1950s, if someone I knew needed to tell me something, wouldn't they have just called me? Emailed me if they needed me to have a physical copy of it?

That meant this couldn't be good.

There was no reason for this guy to have a packet with my name on it. I swivelled back around and looked at the bell hop. He was still smiling.

"For me?" I asked again. "Because I wasn't expecting anything," I added.

"*Si*," he said again and nodded. "*Per te*."

"Are you sure?"

"*Si*," he said tilting his head slightly to the side, his smile never wavering.

I slowly stuck my hand through the small gap in the door and took the envelope between the edges of my fingertips.

"*Grazie*," I said.

He nodded. "*Prego*," he said, hesitating before he walked away.

I pushed the door closed and locked it. Walking briskly across the room, I tossed the envelope onto one of the queen-sized beds then backed up. I didn't stop until I had landed against the wall. Teeth gnawing on bottom lip, I sat down in the window seat and stared at it.

"What if there's anthrax in that envelope?" I posed my question aloud. I looked down at my fingers. "Maybe I should wash my hands."

I'd seen plenty of *Forensic Files* shows where murderers just killed random people I thought as I went into the bathroom. I scrubbed my hands with soap and let the steamy hot water run over them. "For no reason at all," I muttered as I dried them on a towel. And people traveling by themselves . . . It was just as if they had a target on their back.

I stared at my reflection in the mirror—I was all by myself.

That part I never would have dreamt I'd be doing.

My boyfriend, okay, now ex-boyfriend, Kenneth "Gator" Brown had dumped me. He did it right before our trip to Rio De Janeiro. The one where I was sure he was going to propose.

My mother had warned me about him. "Arrogant and cocky," she had said, and, she shook her head piteously, sure to break my heart.

I hated it when she was right.

Kenneth had plenty of reasons to be like he was, no one could deny that. Good looking. Beautiful smile. Smooth chocolate brown skin. He always smelled good and had muscles jumping out everywhere. He'd been the star football player and wrestler in high school. So yeah, he had cause to think highly of himself.

But the voice of reason, my mother, didn't skip a beat reminding me that he'd been out of high school for ten years and he hadn't done anything noteworthy since.

"And, he works at the Super 10," she'd added.

"I know, Mama, but he's the manager. That's good, right?"

"Good for nothing," she quipped. Being upper management at a discount store didn't impress my mother one iota. "And why does he have the nickname Gator?" she'd continue. "The boy was born and raised in Tallahassee. Not an alligator in sight."

That much was true . . .

So, I hadn't told her the part about him dumping me. Didn't want to hear any I told you so's.

Instead, I thanked God we'd gotten refundable tickets and that I was the one holding on to them. As soon as I got over my first bout of sobbing, I marched myself right back to where I had purchased them to get my money back.

But now staring at the brown envelope on the bed and thinking it may be the last few minutes of my life, I wished I had come clean to my mother about Kenneth and me. She probably would have spouted words of wisdom, consoled me, and made me realize that I didn't need to run away to some foreign country because that wouldn't make my hurt feelings go away. If I had just spoken to her about it, I was sure I wouldn't be in this predicament right now.

Guess I could have just told myself that . . .

But the decision to go away to nurse my wounds, wasn't all my idea. The travel agent—I know now her intentions were selfish, not wanting to lose the commission—helped me book a make-me-feel-better trip to Rome.

Yes, I had a travel agent. She may have secured everything online like most people do nowadays, but I was not one to use the internet. I'd heard all about the horror stories of non-secure sites where people's identities were stolen. It was as bad as punching in your social security number over the phone. And swiping a credit card at the gas station pump was another thing. . . Oh, don't get me started.

Now, I had to worry about mysterious envelopes appearing out of nowhere from God knows who, containing God knows what.

Okay, so it was only one envelope, but that just might be all it took.

I looked at it laying innocuously on my bed. No alarms. No sign of caution. It just sitting there expecting me to unwittingly open it, take a whiff and fall over dead.

Ugh!

I should have done what Angie had told me to do, maybe I wouldn't be sitting here moments away from being a casualty of tourism.

Angie Sinclair Abbott, my travel agent, had told me traveling alone wasn't bad and if I felt uncomfortable, which I usually did, just to build a backstory to share with people I met along the way.

"A *fake* one," she emphasized as she pushed those over-sized glasses up her nose. "It'll give you confidence. You won't have to let anyone know who you really are and you'll feel much safer."

That had seemed like total nonsense to me, and not in the least bit legal. I just couldn't imagine taking such advice from a woman who didn't even know how to buy the right sized glasses to fit her face. She was constantly pushing on them. And I just knew if had I followed her lead, she'd probably be looking through those black rimmed spectacles at a mugshot of my face splattered all over the local newspapers back home in Florida. The headline reading: *Kindergarten Teacher Charged with Identity Fraud.*

If there were such a thing.

I was sure there was. So I hadn't listened to her. Maybe now, looking at that envelope, that was a bad move on my part . . .

I flapped my arms, slapping my hands down on my knees and popped up. "What is wrong with me?" I muttered. Gloom and doom swirling in my head all over a stupid envelope." I sucked my tongue. "I haven't even looked at the thing."

So I decided to look at it.

I sidled up next to the bed where I'd dropped the envelope and peeked at the return address. As soon as I saw it I jumped back from the bed and fell over backwards onto the other one. I smacked my hand against my chest and gasped. I couldn't believe what it said.

The return address was Rio De Janeiro.

OMG!

I laid back on the bed, my head suddenly feeling heavy. My heart beating fast. My lips dry. Trying to muster up enough saliva to swallow, I rolled over on my side, my back to the envelope and took in a breath.

Who could have sent me a letter from Rio?

I started shaking my head. Someone was taunting me. Someone was toying with me. It had to be.

But who?

I hadn't told anyone I was coming to Italy except for my mother.

And of course, the travel agent knew.

Wait . . . I did tell the postman . . . and my father . . . and my neighbor, Mrs. Pratt.

Oh geesh.

But no one knew I had originally planned on going to Rio. Well, except my mother . . .

And the travel agent, the postman, my father and my neighbor, Mrs. Pratt.

Shoot!

There was no telling how many people they'd told. I turned over, pushed my thick red hair out of my eyes and glared at the envelope.

This was just making me too nervous. I sat up on the side of the bed, snatched my phone from the nightstand, stabbed in the password and scrolled through my recent calls and texts. There was nothing. No calls. No texts. Nothing about anyone sending me a packet.

"Why are you here?" I sneered at it. "What is it you have to tell me?"

Open me up and see . . .

"Okay." I swallowed. "I will." I took in a breath and held it. I reached over and gingerly picked up the envelope.

Well . . .

"Yeah, yeah," I muttered. "I'm opening it." I tore open the flap and peered inside. No white powder.

Thank God.

Inside was a sheet of white paper folded around something. I slid it out, opened it and found a note. Inside the paper was a hotel room key and a single airline ticket. My eyes scurried across the face of the ticket taking in all the information.

Passenger: Bell/Rowan Miss
From: Rome FCO
To: Rio de Janeiro GIG

Whoa! Wait a minute.

I turned my eyes to the note, with hands shaking I tried to steady myself to read it. It said: *Let's pick up things where we left off.*

It was signed *-G*

"G?" I scrunched up my face, and then a realization came over me. "G for Gator?"

No. Couldn't be. I let my eyes drift off and thought about that idea. I never had called him that. I always called him Kenneth.

But who else could it be?

And—I started feeling butterflies in my stomach--hadn't he said, the day he told me it was quits, that we might "pick" things up again? That he just needed time.

Yes! He'd said that.

So . . . was that what this note was telling me now?

A smile curled up the sides of my mouth and my heart picked up another beat, beginning to thump excitedly.

Had to be. I reread the note. Again. Then again.

Let's pick up things where we left off . . .

And wasn't where we "left off" being engaged. I bounced my head around letting that thought gel. Well . . . *almost* engaged.

Yes! It was.

I looked at the note—only thing was, why would he sign it that way?

It didn't matter. It was him.

Kenneth wanted to get back together!

He wanted to make up.

He wanted me to come to Rio to be with him, and I didn't give anything else a second thought.

I looked at the ticket. Departure time was at nine forty. I checked my watch. Six forty-five.

Crap!

I'd have to hurry if I was going to have enough time to get through security and catch my flight. I went into warp drive. After that everything became a blur. I was out of the hotel and on my plane faster than Floridians buy bottled water after a hurricane warning.

I had called down to the front desk and told them I was checking out. "Send up a cart. Get me a shuttle. I have a plane to catch!" I told them.

I threw all my clothes into my suitcase. To heck with folding. I ran in the bathroom, brushed my teeth and put my hair into a ponytail and raked all my toiletries over into the bag and headed back into the bedroom. Then I dumped everything out of my suitcase and folded them neatly before placing them back.

No need of being too reckless.

I put on a pair of pants and pulled a t-shirt over my head. By the time I was sticking my feet into my sandals, another knock came from the door. This time, I didn't hesitate to answer.

I swung the door wide open. "*Buongiorno*," I chirped with a huge grin across my face. "I'm ready to go. I just need to grab my purse."

"Is that your bag?" a different bell hop, one evidently that knew English, asked.

"Yep," I said. I grabbed my purse and floated down the hallway not even once glancing back. Moving forward was all I was concerned about. Getting to Kenneth.

To Gator . . .

I had been staying at the Hotel *Raffaello* while in Italy. Beautiful. Immersed in culture and history. Plastered in the heart of the city, it had stolen mine. Yes. I had enjoyed my stay and had been looking forward to the remaining days left in my tour package. The majestic eternal city steeped in legend and mythology had captivated me, drawn me in and put to the back of my mind my troubling love life. I savoured the food, the wine, the anachronistic patchwork of old and new—piazzas, open-air markets surrounded by ancient monuments.

But there was no remorse in leaving early. A hasty decision to be sure, but not one, I assured myself, I'd ever regret.

And truly I felt that way all the way to the point where I used my mailed room key to open Suite 304 at the Casa Nova Hotel on *Rua do Riachuelo* in Rio and saw blood.

Chapter Two

The blood was smeared on the wall near the door, and it covered a towel that sat right in the midst of my path into the room. I covered my mouth to muffle the scream. I jerked my hand off the doorknob afraid it too might be covered in blood.

Kenneth was all I could think of. He was here waiting for me, and now . . . *Oh my God!*

Could it be him?

I didn't know what to do. Should I go in? Maybe he was still alive and needed my help. But what if the attacker, or plural, *attackers,* were still in the room?

My breathing was rapid, I squeezed tears out of my eyes and still hadn't taken my hand away from my mouth. I parked my suitcase at the door and sat my purse on top of it then took one step in and then another. I got as far as the bathroom, just to the left of the door and saw bare feet sticking out between the two beds. Bare feet. And they weren't moving.

I stopped and listened. There were no sounds. Nothing that made me think that anyone else was in that room. I turned my head, adjusting my ear closer to the interior. There was no moaning or crying. No breathing noises. That made me think that the guy on the floor was either unconscious or ... dead.

I bent over, holding my stomach. I felt as if I was going to spew all that celebratory white wine I'd drank on the plane ...

Sniffing back the tears, bottom lip trembling, I moved my hand from mouth to stomach. I tried to stand up straight.

Push myself forward. Yes, I know, it was a strange thing for me to do. But even with all of my idiosyncrasies, I had to see whose body was attached to those feet.

The skin not as dark as I thought Kenneth's should be, but they were definitely brown. And from the size, they definitely belonged to a man.

That was when the blubbering started. Me blubbering. I just knew, in my gut, that the person lying there was Kenneth.

I inched one foot across the carpet then dragged the other. I blew out a breath ready to try it again. But something told me to look behind me, so I did. I had left the door standing wide open.

Crap!

If anyone passed by it, they'd see me.

I should have shut it.

I *should have* ran and called the police. That was what I should have done when I first opened the door. That would have been the smart thing to do. It was what I told my kindergarteners to do. I always taught them if you see something or someone bad, run! Run away as fast as you can. Scream as loud as you can! Run! Scream! Run!

But I hadn't done that. How silly of me. I had walked right into the lion's den and now I couldn't go back to shut the door. If I did, I knew I wouldn't come back to see who was lying on the floor, and I needed to know for sure that it was Kenneth.

Curiosity, it seemed, was stronger than any innate fears I had.

Trembling, tears nearly clouding my view, I drew in a breath and forced my foot to take a bigger step, I let the other follow. I stretched my neck and tried to peer over the bed, but everything was a blur. I swiped my eyes and knew with all my bawling, I wasn't going to be able to make out anything.

Ugh! I needed to get closer. I looked down at my legs. My feet felt like they were filled with lead and my knees had turned to rubber. To compensate, and keep me going forward, I got down on my knees. I figured with the help of my hands, I could get farther along. Plus, I thought with my murky reasoning, if I were low, perhaps someone walking down the hall wouldn't immediately notice me.

Although anyone within a hundred-foot radius would detect my sobbing.

So, I crawled. Hand and knee I made my way over to the bed, creeping in fear of what I was bound to find.

My 12-hour, non-stop flight to Rio de Janeiro had felt evanescent compared to the time it was taking me to move twenty-feet, just to the end of the bed. I had glided off that plane, not wanting to waste time in seeing Kenneth.

Then I saw Kenneth.

It was him. He was dead! Oh my, God! My God. He was dead.

I fell against the bed, on the verge of retching, tears filling up in my eyes, I knew I had to get out of there.

I got up and stumbled out of the room and down the hall way, slinging my purse over my shoulder and dragging my suitcase behind me. Then I stumbled back to the room. I covered my hand with my t-shirt and grabbed the doorknob shutting the door.

I rounded the corner of the hallway to get to the elevator. Head down trying to control my sobs long enough to get out of there, my feet one in front of the other moving instinctively. I just felt numb. My mind was racing.

How would I make it without him? What could I say to his parents? Who did this to him and why?

I knew I needed to call the police. His death definitely wasn't of natural causes. I also knew I'd have to come back and identify his body. I was the only one in Brazil who could do that. I wasn't sure how I was going to make it through that, but right now, I knew that I needed some air.

Bam!

I ran right smack into some guy, tumbled back and almost fell onto the floor. He grabbed me, whiffs of an earthy rosewood scent wafted up my nose. It was woody. Aromatic.

"Oh," I said, never lifting up my head. I sniffed back tears. "Excuse me. Sorry." I tried to get around him, but he was gently holding onto my arm.

"Are you okay?" he asked.

I pulled my arm away from his grasp. I looked up into his face, back down the hallway where to I had come from and then back at him.

My thoughts were jumbled, certainly, but his actions suddenly seemed suspicious to me—holding onto me, asking me questions as if he knew who I was.

Who was he?

I too another gander back toward the room where I'd left Kenneth. I didn't know this man, there was no reason for him to hold onto me and he was heading in the direction of a room where I knew for a fact a man had just been murdered. My man. I decided it was time to take heed to what I'd always told my kindergarteners. Screaming, I pushed him aside and I ran.

I ran right past the open elevator doors, and ran down the two flights of steps, my suitcase bumping along behind me and I ran out into the streets.

The day was clear. The late afternoon sun was bright. The streets were filled with people and cars and noises. Lots of noises, and enough people to get lost in. But I wasn't finished running. I ran across the street and down a block where I saw a sign that I could read. One in English *The Watering Hole* was scrawled in big brown letters across an aged wooden plank that hung over the door by a wrought iron bracket. I peered in through the small window on the door, it looked dark enough for me to hide out in until I could get help.

I gave the door a push and stepped inside, the smell of beer and alcohol slamming me in my face overtaking my senses. I tried to stand up straight—look like I hadn't just seen my boyfriend, uh fiancé's body. I swiped my hands over my eyes to clear them, and scanned the place.

"Restroom," in red neon *and* in English pointed me toward the back of the bar. I didn't let my sight wander, I kept it straight ahead and took off for the toilet.

Once inside, I locked the door behind me and looked at my reflection in the mirror. My face was so red that my freckles blended in and was almost the same color as my now unkempt-looking hair. And my eyes showed no contrast.

"What is going on?" I spoke to my reflection. "Why is this happening?"

I blew out a breath and turned on the cold water. I threw some on my face, grabbed a couple of paper towels, and putting the toilet seat down, I sat and held the napkins over my face.

I just wanted to break down and cry. I wanted to call my mother. Tell her and Daddy to come and get me. That I would wait right in this stall until they got to me.

Knock. Knock.

I jumped. Then blew out a breath, it was only someone wanting to get in.

"It's occupied," I responded to the tap on the door. "I'll be out in a minute."

Guess I can't sit here as long as I hoped, I thought. Then out loud, "Plus," I blew my nose on the paper towel, "I have to make sure someone sees about Kenneth."

I ran the towel over my eyes again, threw it in the trash and unlocked the door. I peered out, making sure that guy hadn't followed me, then located a dark corner booth to sit in.

It was time to call the police.

I pulled my cell phone out of my shoulder bag and stared at it. Did they have 911 in Rio? I sniffed, swiped my hand across my nose and thought. Maybe I could google how to call the police.

"I thought I was having a bad day, but you look like yours was a hundred times worse than mine."

I looked up to see a woman standing over me. She held a glass of red wine in her hand and was wiping a wet cloth over her blouse. I smiled at her.

"Are you okay?" she asked. "I haven't seen you in here before, you look kind of lost."

I stared at her, the wet rag leaving streaks across her shirt. She took a gulp of the wine waiting, it seemed, for me to answer.

"Mind if I sit down," she said and nodded to the other bench in the booth.

Yes, I mind! was what I was thinking, "No. Please sit down," was what I said.

What was I supposed to say?

"I spilled wine on my blouse," she said as she scooted into the bench. "Couldn't get the wine in me fast enough." She licked her lips. "Just wanted to drown out today's craziness." She took another gulp. "You want a drink?"

"No," I said.

I turned and looked at the bar and all the people around it. An older woman was behind it, serving up drinks, snatching up money off the counter sticking it in the register and laughing it up with her customers. I heard voices and word floating around and for the first time, I noticed that everyone was speaking English.

Wasn't I in a county where the people spoke Portuguese?

"You speak English?" I turned back and asked her.

"Yeah, I do," she said and giggled. "This is an expats' bar. Most of us gave up on our country, but not on the language. Everyone here speaks English."

I slowly nodded my head. No wonder the signs were in English. And what luck, surely someone here could help me get the police.

"I'm Enid, by the way," the woman said and stuck out her hand for me to shake.

I took her hand and shook it. "Rebecca," I lied. "Rebecca Fontaine." Figured it was time to take bespectacled Angie, the travel agent's advice. I didn't want anyone here knowing my name so later they could place me at the hotel before I had had a chance to speak to the police and get my side of the story out. I just hoped Miss Enid didn't ask for any "backstory" because I hadn't thought that far ahead.

"Nice to meet you, Rebecca Fontaine." She smiled at me. "Now that we're acquainted, you wanna tell me what's going on with you? I worry about my fellow Americans, especially women, walking around alone down here."

"Down where?"

"Rio de Janeiro," she said and spread out her arms. "That's where you are, isn't it?" She chuckled. "In case you forgot to read your tourist brochure, this is not the safest place to be."

"How do you know I'm all alone?"

"We saw you when you walked in." She nodded her head toward the door. "You went straight to the restroom, eyes all red. We could tell you'd been crying."

"Who is we?"

She raised her eyebrows and gestured around the room. "We're all a big family here. We stick together."

"Enid," I started slowly. Hesitating to share anything about what I'd seen or even how I felt. This woman's words had made me feel better, and I was happy to be in the company of Americans. Still, I wondered if I could trust her. Or anyone. My eyes drifted around the room.

The woman behind the bar appeared to be in her mid-fifties. She had on an old men's cardigan that was too big for her small body. Her shoulder length hair was blonde-going-gray and was beginning to get straggly. She'd lean over the bar, speak to her customers, then turn away to get what they wanted. She didn't seem to care much about anything.

Everyone else was in their own world. One or two people talked with one another, others sat nursing their drinks, glancing up at the television, or talking on their cell phones.

I turned back to look at Enid and let out a sigh. I realized I didn't have much choice. I had to trust someone.

"I need to call the police. Can you help me with that?"

"Something really bad is wrong, huh?"

"No." I swallowed hard. "Not with me. But . . ."

She held up her hand. "No need to tell me anything, Rebecca, if it's going to upset you. But the police around here aren't . . . Let me see . . . How should I put this . . . Helpful."

"No?"

"No. Best bet, if you need help, is to go to the Embassy."

"The embassy?" I asked her. "The American Embassy?"

"Yep," she nodded. "I can take you there, if you'd like. Just have to pay my tab." She downed the rest of her drink and used the glass to point toward the bar.

"Rowan?" I felt someone standing over me and I knew who it was even before I looked up. I could smell his rosewood cologne.

Hallway Man.

The guy I ran into in the hallway at the hotel had somehow found me.

Startled and confused, I almost peed on myself.

How did he know my name? How did he find me? And what had he come to do to me? My hands started trembling and my eyes secretly searched for a way out.

"Rowan?" Enid said. "No. That's not her name. Her name's Rebecca Fontaine."

"Rowan Bell." It was a different male voice saying my name this time, one that had an accent. Stepping from behind Hallway Man, a uniformed police officer looked down at me. "*Senhorita* Bell," he said. "I need you to come with me, *por favor*."

Chapter Three

"Please, have a seat," the police officer said as he ushered me around an office full of desks. He'd made me leave my luggage at the Watering Hole, but he hadn't handcuffed me. And his tone, even now and during the entire ride over to the police station from the bar, seemed quite polite. He'd spoken to me in English and even walked away and left after getting me into a chair.

"I need you to fill out this form, *por favor*," he said. "Personal information so we can contact you if we need to."

His niceness, I decided, must be to dupe me into submission. To get me to confess so they could quickly wrap this up. Charge me with Kenneth's murder and execute me for a capital offense. I'd heard about things just like that on the *ID Channel*. And I knew being found guilty in a foreign country didn't take much. Such governments didn't hesitate on handing down the death penalty to American citizens. Hadn't Enid just warned me that the police in Rio weren't helpful?

Yes, she had!

Oh my God!

And didn't they use firing squads here? I swiveled this way and that in my seat and frantically eyeballed the room. Filled with police officers, guns everywhere, no way to escape, I was a sitting duck. Did any of them speak English? I strained my ear and listened. Yep! They were all speaking Portuguese. Would my Spanish get me by? Or, had my only hope to be understood just left? Would I be able to explain to them what happened? Would I even be given the opportunity? I felt tears welling up in my eyes.

I should have gotten that *Portuguese for Dummies* book I saw in the airport. I had just figured Portuguese was close to Spanish, a language one couldn't live in Florida without some basic knowledge of. And of course there wouldn't be much need to talk because I'd be with Kenneth . . .

Poor Kenneth.

Now he was dead and they were going to put me in front of a firing squad for killing him!

I glanced down at the form. It had the instructions in both Portuguese and English. I read over before I started filling in the blanks, to see what kind of "personal information" they needed. Name. Address. Phone number. Contact information.

As I wrote, I wondered should I give them truthful information. Angie's advice was whispering in my ear . . . *Use a fake identity . . .*

That hadn't worked so well with Enid.

I filled out the form and pushed it aside, hoping that would trigger someone to pay attention to me and get me the heck out of there. I glanced around the room to see if anyone was patiently waiting by for me to finish. But they were all doing their own thing. Then I saw Hallway Man walk in the door.

What was he doing here?

I watched through the glass partition as he sauntered over to an office and walked in without even hesitating or knocking. He gestured with his hands, animatedly speaking.

Was he talking about me?

That couldn't be good.

Argh!

I just wanted to leave. Get out of there. Get out of Rio. Out of Brazil. I didn't know how much a same day ticket would cost, and I didn't care. I patted my purse, my bank card and my passport were inside. All I had to do was get out of that door.

I glanced over at the door. A red sign that read: *Saída* greeted me.

Exit! My passage out.

My eyes darted around the room. No one seemed to be paying attention to me. They were all busy at their desks or talking with real criminals. So I eased up out of my chair.

No one even looked up.

I sidestepped away from the desk.

Not one of those police officers moved.

I tiptoed backwards to the archway toward the hall and that exit sign.

Not one peep from *la policía*.

I was almost out. I looked toward the office that Hallway Man had gone into and it seemed like he looked directly at me. I jumped behind the wall to hide.

I held my breath waiting for him to appear in front of me, accusing me of murder, but nothing happened. I glanced at the exit, then peeked around the corner to the office. The door was ajar, and listening intently I could hear that they were speaking in Portuguese. I couldn't understand one word of what they were saying. My coveted Spanish comprehension had just gone out the window.

Guess Portuguese wasn't as much like Spanish as I thought.

I glanced over at the person Hallway Man was talking to—a tall, mid-fortyish guy in a suit.

Suit Guy looked official. Maybe a plain clothes detective. Then again, he had his own office. Maybe he was the chief of police.

Egad!

I held my breath and watched them as they talked, nodding, seemingly in agreement, then they both turned and looked my way. At least in the direction I should have been. At that chair.

Should I run back over and slide into it? Stay put and hope they hadn't notice that seconds before it'd been empty?

That was definitely the mentality of a kindergartner and not the teacher.

Crap!

I decided to stay put. That was probably the best idea. I shrank down making myself one with the wall. I closed my eyes and silently prayed for the power of invisibility to suddenly manifest. That was probably the only way I was going to get out of this.

I glanced around the corner of the wall and there they stood, still talking. Evidently they hadn't noticed my absence, they were lost in conversation.

Maybe I kept imaging that they were looking at me.

But that prolonged conversation was worrying me. It had to be about me, right? I mean what other reason would they detain me? Plus, the only thing I had in common with Hallway Man was the encounter at the hotel. It was the only reason I even knew him.

Well, actually, I didn't *know* him . . .

Then I wondered how did Hallway Man know me? He knew my name. Knew where to find me. Was he coming to my room when I bumped into him to see me?

I hadn't checked in, but someone had to know I was coming. Someone other than Kenneth. Or worse, had Kenneth, desperate to save his life told his killer he was expecting me hoping that would cause them to flee leaving him unharmed and unwittingly caused the killers to lay-in-wait to ambush me?

Poor Kenneth . . .

Did Hallway Man know Kenneth?

Wait . . . I gasped, my eyes getting as wide as saucers. Is he the one who killed Kenneth?

Oh Lord!

Now I knew what this was about. I knew, without understanding one thing being said what was going on.

Hallway Man was setting me up.

For capital murder.

Hallway Man was putting the blame on me!

Oh my, Lord! I was going down. The Brazilian government was going to throw me in prison then execute me for a crime I didn't commit.

Who would believe me? Everyone in jail claims they didn't do it. I would just be another innocent prisoner.

That gave me all the courage I needed to bolt for the door.

"Hold on, *Senhorita*," Suit Man said catching me by my arm before I could make it to the door. "Where are you heading in such a hurry?"

Now they leave the office . . .

"I need my phone call!" I blurted out the words as I turned to face him. I had decided it was time to call my mother. "It's my right!" I said, my eyes locked with his. "I have rights you know."

"What rights are those, *Senhorita*?" Suit Man said almost mockingly

"Oh God!" I said muttering, hanging my head. Fifth. Fourth. Sixth Amendment. Heck, I didn't know. And me being way down in South America, did I even have rights? So I changed my tune. "I want to talk to someone at the Embassy," I said. "The American Embassy."

Spouses and significant others were always the prime suspect in cases like this (I knew that because of the show *Fatal Attractions*). And even though Kenneth and I had broken up, we were on the mend. But they might not know that, that made this a high profile case. It made sense to get the full force of the American government behind me.

"Why don't we just sit down and talk?" Suit Man said.

"Talk?" My throat went dry. I knew this was how they got the confession. They lock you in a room with dim lights, try to get your DNA off of Coke cans that they've forced you to drink from and then put words in your mouth.

"Yes," he said, a little smile showing under his black moustache.

"I didn't kill Kenneth," I said, may as well let him know he wasn't going to get a false confession out of me. "And you can't make me say I did. It wasn't me. I didn't kill him."

"You didn't kill Kenneth?" he said, his eyebrows arching upward.

"No! Emphatically, adamantly, no!" I said. "You have no evidence. You won't be able to pin *that* one on me."

"I see," he said nodding, a sly smile on his face. "Well that's good, no?" He looked down at me. "But tell me this . . ." he took my arm and led me back toward the chair the first officer had sat me in. ". . . What about the murder of Gerson Crawford? The man found murdered in the room where you were registered. Do you think, maybe," he wobbled his head back and forth, "I can pin *that* one on you?"

Chapter Four

"Gear . . . What? Who?" I stumbled over my words, confused. I didn't know what Suit Guy was talking about. All I knew was that I didn't want *any* murder pinned on me.

"Gerson," he said it phonetically. I guessed to help me grasp the correct pronunciation.

"I don't know a *Gear-son*," I mimicked his intonation and accent.

"Okay," he said. "Well, Mr. Crawford—Gerson—was killed today. I think perhaps you saw him?"

"I saw Kenneth."

"Yes," he said, then gestured for me to sit. "Tell me about Kenneth. Is he dead, too?"

"Yes! He was in my hotel room. And I didn't kill him."

"So you have told me." He took a notebook out of his suit jacket pocket and scrawled something in it. "But the man in your hotel room was not named Kenneth. His name, as I have said, was Gerson Crawford."

It took no time for him to notice the puzzled look on my face.

"Let's start over, shall we?" he said.

I suddenly felt as if he was patronizing me.

"And forgive me for not introducing myself," he continued, not changing his manner of speaking. "I am Detective Jorge Batista, I should have told you that first thing. I work in homicide, as you may have guessed. And you are Rowan Bell, yes?"

"How do you know my name?" I asked.

"Ah, that goes right to my next question." He spoke as if this were a game and I was a five-year-old.

Ha! He couldn't get me there. I knew how to speak kindergarten-ese fluently.

"Questions are good," I said in my schoolteacher voice. I bent forward and made sure I looked at him as I spoke, just like I told my kids. "What question do you have?"

He chuckled. "Ah-ha. I bet you are a favorite for your little students at Ruediger Elementary."

I gasped. How was I going to play his game when he was always one step ahead of me?

"I didn't kill Kenneth," I said flatly. Since I wasn't in his league with the cat-and-mouse game, I just decided to put all my cards on the table. "And I probably shouldn't answer any more of your questions without a lawyer."

"Do you think you need a lawyer?"

"Do you think I killed Kenneth?"

"For that, I don't know. But, while we are on the subject of murder," he said. "I don't think you killed Mr. Crawford. I just want to ask you some questions about him."

I tilted my head to the side. We were back to that guy. The one I didn't know and who evidently was dead—murdered, just like Kenneth.

"How about this?" the detective said, again wasting no time reading my face. "I will tell you what I know." He dipped his head. "Well, the part I *can* tell you. I think that will be best. And then you can tell me what you know." He smiled that sly grin of his. "Deal?"

It seemed like he was up to something. He spoke English too well to be a detective in Brazil, not one hint of Portuguese spilling over into his speech. I could feel he was trying to trick me. It seemed to me that he already knew a lot about me. Exactly what else did he expect me to tell him?

Nothing. There was nothing I could tell him about anything because I didn't know anything, and he knew that.

If I hadn't been so nervous, I would have chuckled to myself because yes, I knew exactly what he was about. It was just as I had thought earlier, bringing up another murder to confuse me and get me to confess to Kenneth's. But it wasn't going to work.

"What do you know?" I said to him, fully intending *not* to tell him anything I knew until I got a lawyer.

"I know that Mr. Crawford sent you a plane ticket and a key to a hotel room he'd reserved for you to Rome."

"No he didn't."

"No?" His eyebrows arched up again and he ran his fingers over his moustache. "Perhaps I am mistaken."

"You are," I said.

"I will continue anyway, okay?"

I nodded. Finally, he didn't have something right—that made me smile.

"And I know that when you arrived," he continued, "without stopping at the front desk of the Casa Nova Hotel, you went straight up to Room 304 and found Mr. Crawford dead between the beds."

Now I understood. Kenneth must've used a fake name to register at the hotel. Maybe he'd been talking to Miss-Fake-Backstory-Angie the travel agent, too.

"His name is—was Kenneth Brown," I said, happy to correct Mr. Know-It-All-Detective. "He was my fiancé."

"Who?" He let his lips stay in the "o" position.

"Kenneth."

"The other dead guy?" He swung his finger to the right as if pointing to someone else.

"The only dead guy."

"Ah, now I see." He scrawled something in his notebook. "You think the person in your hotel room was this Kenneth Brown."

"It was."

He made a short humming sound under his breath and shook his head. He batted his eyes. "No. It was not. You are mistaken."

"I don't think it is me that's mistaken," I said.

"Did you look at the body?"

"Yes. I did," I said forcefully. Then I thought about it. Me, blubbering, crawling around on the floor. I did remember that my eyesight was blurry thanks to the flood of tears gushing out. And, I had noticed that Dead Guy's feet weren't as dark as Kenneth's should be. Still I should know my fiancé when I see him, right?

Not so sure about that, Rowan. You don't have the "fiancé" part right, so maybe . . .

Hmmmm.

"So, that wasn't my fia—boyfri . . . Uhm, Kenneth on the floor dead?" I asked.

"Not in that hotel room," he said. "Room 304 at the Casa Nova? No. Did you see him dead somewhere else?"

I shook my head then stuck up a finger, telling the detective to hold on. I fished my cell phone out of my purse and scrolled through my contacts, finding the one I wanted, I pressed "Call."

The phone rang about five times before he picked up.

"Thought you were in Rome, Rowan. Having a good time."

"I am," I said.

Kenneth's voice was dry, not even a "Hello, how you doing?" He didn't seem to know I was in Rio. He did know I had gone to Rome, though. So maybe it had been him who sent me the note. "Did you send me a letter?" I asked him. "Signed it 'G'?"

"What? No," he said, his words curt.

"With a hotel room key?"

"Look Rowan," he said brusquely. "I've moved on with my life. You should, too." And with that he ended the call.

I blew out a breath. I had to blink my eyes to stop the blubbering from starting up again. I didn't know if I felt the sting of tears because I was relieved he wasn't dead, or because at that moment I wished he were.

"Was that Kenneth?" the detective asked. He leaned in toward me as if we were sharing a secret.

"Yes," I said. "Kenneth."

"So, alive?" He hunched his shoulder.

"Yes," I said. "Alive."

"Good." Detective Batista gave a firm nod and sat back in his seat. "No need to go looking for another dead body then."

"But then I don't understand why I'm here."

"At the police station?" he asked.

"In Rio."

"Oh. I do know the answer to that one," he said.

It figures.

"You are here," he said, "because, Mr. Crawford sent for you."

"No. He didn't . . . I mean . . . I don't know . . . ." My eyes drifted to a spot on the wall. Could it be? The realization hitting me. "Gerson," I whispered. "Is he 'G?'"

"Yes," the detective responded although I wasn't speaking to him. "G is for Gerson. Gerson sent for you. He sent the hotel key and the airline ticket. This is what I have been telling you."

I swiped my hand across my forehead. "Why? Why would *he* send for me?" I asked. "How did he even know me?" I brought my eyes around to his, begging him to help me understand.

"I think he brought you here to help him with a murder," Detective Batista said, then nodded his head. "Yes, for this I am almost certain."

I stretched my eyes. "*His* murder? He wanted me to help him with his own murder?"

"Oh no," Detective Batista said, his eyes lighting up as if I'd told him a joke. "He wanted your help with the one *he* committed back in Florida."

Chapter Five

"Allegedly," a deep voice coming from behind me said. I turned to look and found Hallway Man standing a few feet away. "Allegedly, he committed a murder back in Florida," he said. He stepped next to me and I could smell his cologne. Again. It was woody. Aromatic. Fetching. And it was beginning to drive me crazy.

Hallway Man was tall. Very tall. Mocha-colored skin, jet-black hair, a sexy stubble down his jawline and around his mouth.

Wait . . . Did I say sexy?

I didn't mean sexy. Sexy people can't be annoying and he was definitely annoying me.

Why was he butting in to the conversation? I looked up at him. Didn't anyone speak Portuguese around here? He didn't have an accent either. I narrowed my eyes at him.. I needed to figure out who he was and what he wanted.

"Ah. Yes," Detective Batista said standing up. "Your kind is fond of that word."

Hallway Man didn't seem to appreciate that comment. He blew out a breath and closed his eyes momentarily.

"I'm leaving," Hallway Man said. "Just thought I'd let you know."

"Take her with you," Detective Batista said and pointed at me with a nod of his head. "I have no more questions for her."

"I had planned to," Hallway Man said. "I wouldn't leave her to fend for herself, all alone."

"I'm not going with him," I said, my brow knitted in frustration. "I don't even know him."

"You don't know him either, huh?" The police detective asked with a smirk. He swiped his moustache then looked at Hallway Man. "She doesn't know the deceased isn't Kenneth. She doesn't know your brother. She doesn't know you. I'm not even sure if she knows her own name. How did you think she was going to be of any help?"

"Brother?" I looked at Hallway Man. "*My* name?" I turned and looked at the detective. Oh, my God. I was getting more frustrated by the minute. "Just hold on." I popped up out of my seat. "My name *is* Rowan Bell. You already know that. So maybe it's you that's mixed up."

"Ah," the detective said. "But didn't you tell someone at the Watering Hole your name was something else? Let me see . . ." He picked up his notebook and flipped through it. "Yes. Here it is. Rebecca Fontaine. Is that you?" He shrugged. "You can see what I mean." He looked at Hallway Man shaking his head.

Argh!

The detective's entire demeanor had changed. He now seemed uncooperative and dismissive. He knew my name. My *real* name. No reason to hash through an explanation with him about that *faux pas*. So I turned to "Brother."

"Whose brother are you?" I asked Hallway Man.

"I'm Gerson's brother," he said.

"Don't be confused," Detective Batista said mockingly. "He is not speaking about Kenneth." He put a big emphasis on the name.

"Who is Kenneth?" Gerson's brother asked.

"Take her, Enes," Detective Batista said.

Oh, Hallway Man's name is Enes . . .

But don't let her leave Rio," he continued, "I may need to talk to her again. Although, so far she seems useless. I don't know what Gerson was thinking."

"What?" Slow to get what he was saying, it hit me. I swung back around and looked at the moustached detective. "I can't leave Rio?" I felt that rush of tears coming back. "I don't think that's right," I said. "Didn't you say you knew I didn't kill Gerson?"

"Yes. I did," the detective said. He'd sat back down at his desk and started going through paperwork. Evidently no more time for me. "This is a murder investigation. I may need you, you are a witness."

"Not to the murder." I sat back in my seat to face him.

"And you have a tie to the victim."

"No I don't," I said. "Other than finding him."

"You didn't find him, his brother did," the detective nodded toward Enes. "And until we get it straightened out what assistance you promised to give and how you fit into all of this, I will need you to stay. And I need you not to say one word about what you saw, although I'm not sure if I can trust your eyes." He smirked.

"What I saw?" I asked.

"What you saw." He gave me a stern look. "No one knows how he died. And if anyone does, then they are probably the killer, or at least knows who did it."

I thought about that. Did I know how he was killed? I nodded. I did. Although his face was down, I could see the big dent in his head. Blood everywhere. He must have been hit more than once.

"Hey," he squinted his eyes and pointed his finger at me trying to get my attention. I was lost in thought. "You may not be a murderer, *senhorita*," he said, "but I don't think you are a very honest person. But I am going to trust you not to speak about this." He turned back to his work, mumbling. "All of this Kenneth nonsense. *Louco*."

"I know what that means," I said. "And I don't think you can keep me here. In Rio." I swallowed hard. "Especially if you know I've done nothing wrong. Just because I was mistaken on the identity of the victim." I crossed my arms over my chest, mustering up much more bravado then I ever thought possible. "I think I need a lawyer. An American lawyer."

"There you go," Detective Batista said and swung his finger toward the brother. "Attorney Enes Crawford. An American. Just like you. Licensed to practice in Florida. Just where you're from." He turned to Enes. "Now take her from my station." He waved at me telling the both of us, I guessed, that it was time for me to go.

Hmph!

I stood up. Not exactly sure if I wanted to leave with Hallway Man . . . Dead Guy's Brother . . . Mr. Florida Attorney or whoever he was, or not.

Okay, so now I knew his name--Enes Crawford, but it didn't make me feel comfortable being with him. There was a lot going on with him. For one, he knew me. So, why didn't he say something when I bumped into him in the hallway of the hotel? He knew where to find me and he knew that his brother was dead in my hotel room. And he never said a word. I, on the other hand, didn't know anything about him. Like the detective, he was one step ahead of me

"You ready?" he said.

"What?" I realized that after I had stood up, I hadn't moved. During my rumination my feet had stayed firmly planted and I was sure my eyes were glazed over.

"Or do you want to stay here?" Enes asked. My reverie broken, I looked at him and then over at Detective Batista.

What a choice . . .

"I'm ready to go," I said. I put my purse over my shoulder and headed toward the door.

"We will speak again soon," the detective called out, seemingly to taunt me as I opened the door and walked away.

I didn't look back. I didn't want to give him the satisfaction. I just kept walking until I realized I didn't know where I was going.

I turned around and looked at Enes who was a few feet behind me. "I don't know what to do," I said. My arms spread eagle, I started walking backwards. "This doesn't seem real to me. I feel like I'm in Oz or something."

He chuckled. "Believe me, this is not Oz." He pulled out his keys and hit the clicker. "What do you *want* to do?" he asked and turned to go in the opposite direction than I was heading.

"Go home," I said trotting behind him to catch up.

He sighed. "I know what you mean."

I caught up, and walked next to him. "You can't leave either?" I asked.

"I can. And I will. Soon. I have to take my brother home, you know. But I'd like to see if it is possible to find out what happened to him." He blew out a breath. He stopped walking and stood still. "If I'd only gotten there sooner."

"I'm sorry about your brother," I said. I stopped walking too. "But you have to know, I don't know anything about him." I shook my head. "I can't help you, if that's what you're thinking. And I can't help that detective either."

"If you couldn't help him why did you tell him you could?" He started up walking again. Seemingly troubled by what I was saying.

"I don't know what you're talking about," I said.

He looked at me at first, it seemed with contempt, and then his face softened. "This is all so confusing to me. And it seems like, although I don't know why, it's confusing to you, too."

"Oh, it definitely is confusing to me."

"So then, how about if we start from the beginning," he said. "Tell each other what we know. That way we can both get some questions answered."

That was almost the same thing as what the detective had said. At that point, though, I wasn't sure I wanted to know the answer to anything other than when I could go home.

"Do you mind talking to me?" he asked, noticing I hadn't answered him.

"About what?" I asked.

"About my brother. About why you're here."

"That's something I'd like to find out, Enes," I said. "Why I'm here. Do you think you have the answer to that?"

He shrugged. "Some of the answers, I guess. At least I thought I knew. Maybe you can help me fill in the blanks." He looked at me questioningly. "How about . . ." he smiled, seemingly rolling over an idea in his head. "I take you someplace. Just the two of us. Alone. So we can work this out. How about that?"

"Stranger danger," I said. "How about *that*?"

He chuckled. "You're safer with me than you'd be by yourself. Haven't you heard about the crime rate in Rio? Homicides are all too common."

"I'm learning," I said, remembering Enid at the Watering Hole had been the first to enlighten me about crime in Rio. "And, in case you've forgotten, I've seen it first-hand."

Chapter Six

"No rain today," Enes glanced upward. "How about we go and walk along the beach to talk?" He glanced at me and smiled. "It's beautiful there, not too far from the expat community and we'll be surrounded by people."

I chuckled to myself. I guessed he was trying to help me feel safe. "The beach is fine," I said.

We were in his red Fiat Spider convertible. I guessed it was rented. Couldn't imagine him shipping his car across the ocean just to come and visit.

Unless, of course, he was rich and kept a home on both continents.

My glance matched his and I returned the smile.

Rich? I couldn't tell although he was a lawyer. Didn't know if being one made you the other. Nice? I hadn't decided. Wasn't sure whether he was keeping me safe because he wanted information on his brother, something I did *not* have. Or, if he was the type of person that genuinely cared about other people. He smelled good I knew that. It was something I'd noticed from the first moment I bumped into him. And tall. And he was handsome—that was something I had just begun to notice.

"Does it rain a lot here?" I asked, going back to his comment about the weather.

"It does." He nodded. "But not so much in the winter."

"This is summer," I said. My designated vacation time as a schoolteacher. "So it rains more now?"

He smiled at me. "July is winter here. Backwards I know. Come in December, that's summer, then you'll see how much it rains."

Everything in Rio was so backwards. Everybody speaking English, strangers knowing my name, dead guys sending me airline tickets, and detectives detaining me for no reason. I threw my hands up. I'd never gone through anything like this in my life. I hoped I wouldn't ever have to do it again.

"I won't pretend like I'd ever come back here," I said. "I've already had enough of Rio."

Enes threw back his head and laughed.

As we drove to the beach, I soaked in Brazil. It was the first opportunity I had had to slow down and untangle the gray matter in my brain since I'd gotten off the plane.

Sunny skies and a breeze flowing through my hair put a smile on my face. I closed my eyes, leaned back on the headrest, and stuck my hand out of the window. Open palm, letting the wind tap against it, I finally felt the tension of the day dissipating. Early evening had arrived while I'd been held captive at that police station, and now it felt cooler and less humid outside. I had nearly drifted off . . .

Honk! Honk!

I jumped at the sound of horns blowing and opened my eyes. There were cars everywhere. They were swerving through the street, people were hanging out of cars yelling. The traffic was crazy.

"Oh, my," I said.

"This is *Avenida Atlantica*," Enes said it with an accent.

"Wow," I said, sitting up straight. "This beats any traffic jam I've seen on the I-10."

"Traffic is bad down here and drivers are impolite. And even worse around these parts. It's where everyone comes." He pointed past me. "There on your right, that's Copacabana Beach. World famous."

My eyes followed his finger and I saw people everywhere. Toddlers, old folks, and everyone in between—half-dressed—jogging, roller blading, riding on scooters. There were trampolines right there in the street. As we traveled down the road, I could hear music from the cafes and restaurants. I turned to my left and saw the street lined with what looked like upscale hotels.

"We need to find some of the guys," Enes said.

"*The* guys?" I asked, looking around.

"Yeah. For parking. Otherwise, we'll drive around forever looking for a place to park where we won't get ticketed."

"Oh, guys like parking attendants?"

"Yeah, I guess you could call them that. They work for city hall or sometimes for companies that work under concession. They charge you a fee to park, but at least you won't be fined." He pointed. "There's one."

Enes put the top up on the car. We got out, got the ticket from "the guy," and paid him.

"C'mon," he said, putting the ticket on the dashboard. "I'll buy you a coconut to sip on while we walk along the shoreline. It'll make you feel like a true *Carioca*."

He took my arm and guided me over to what looked like a small outdoor bar. He called it a drink stall as we were walking up to it. It had a pointed roof topped with a yellow flag flapping in the wind. All around were round, white tables with bright yellow chairs, and yellow patio umbrellas for shade. We walked up to the counter.

"Like a what?" I asked.

"*Carioca*. That's what people born in Rio are called."

"Oh," I said. "You were born here?"

"Hold on," he said then held up two fingers to the server. He pulled money out of his pocket and placed it on the counter.

After completing his transaction, Enes turned back to me. "I wasn't born here, but Gerson was. So he's a citizen" He hunched a shoulder. "But we still are—were . . . He closed his eyes for a moment and shook his head. "Our mother is Brazilian," he started again. "So I gained Brazilian citizenship because of her. Just the same as if I had been born here."

"Oh," I said.

"Our father is black," he said, sort of out of left field.

I just smiled and nodded my head. I guessed he told me that to show a kinship between the two of us.

He picked up the two coconuts, a paper straw sticking out the top of each and handed me one. I looked down at it, then up at him.

"Try it," he said.

I rolled it around in my hands and examined it. It wasn't brown and furry like the ones I was used to seeing. It was green, with brown bruises around its sides. I put the straw up to my lips and sucked.

"Mmmm," I said. I smiled at him. The water inside had a sweet, nutty flavor. "It's good. I like it."

"Good," he smiled. "I'm glad." He started walking and I followed. "C'mon, let's talk."

I stopped long enough to pull my feet out my sandals and stuff them in my shoulder bag. I felt the warm sand squish between my toes as we started on our walk.

"My father is black, too," I said after a while. I knew I was being facetious, bringing up his statement again, but I couldn't resist. "And so is my mother."

He chuckled and seemed to blush. "I just wanted to let you know."

"So your brother lived here, huh?" I changed the subject, no need of trying to make him feel uncomfortable. I needed answers from him, too.

"No," he said. He took a sip of his coconut. "He *escaped* here. He was a doctor in Tallahassee."

"Really?" I said. It seemed so strange to come this far and find someone from home.

"Yeah. But after he was charged with murder, he had to give up his practice.

And to avoid jail or paying some outrageous bond, he fled here." He looked at me. "Brazil has a no extradition policy for its citizens."

"Oh," I said, nodding, finally understanding one thing out of all the things I had been bombarded with today.

We walked, not saying much and sipped our water. The sun as the backdrop, I could smelled the salt from the ocean, the cool air that wafted across the water, and hear the rush of the soft, foamy waves. There were a few surfers out and people on the beach juggling soccer balls and playing volleyball. But what took me by surprise was that hardly anyone was wearing much of anything.

"People get down to almost the bare nothing to play sports, I see," I said. "A lot of jiggling going around, in every sense of the word."

Enes started to laugh and nearly choked on his water. I saw it come back out of his mouth before he could get a hand up to it.

"That's true," he said, still chuckling. "Brazilians are very serious about their beach sports. And they are very good at them. But out of all the beaches around the world that I've seen, it seems the rule here for women, is less is more." He covered his mouth and coughed to clear his throat. "It's called the 'Brazilian bikini.' You've never heard of it?"

"No." I shook my head. "Never heard of that."

"It's true," he held up his hand as if he were swearing. "Even the men here wear as little as possible."

"I see."

He tucked his head and looked over at me, a sly grin on his face. "Does it make you uncomfortable?"

"I teach kindergarten," I said. "I always tell my kids that everything has to stay inside."

"Kindergarten teacher," he said and shook his head. "I just don't understand that, Rowan."

"Yeah, I've been meaning to ask you. How do you know my name?"

"My brother told me. He told me all about you. Except the part about you being a kindergarten teacher, which makes no sense. But yeah, he conveniently left that part out."

"I didn't know your brother."

A smirk came over his face. "If you didn't know my brother, how did he know your name? Or how to find you in Rome?"

"I don't know," I said. "But I do know that I've never met your brother."

"Then why would you come here to see someone you didn't know?"

"I came to see Kenneth."

"Yeah. Jorge mentioned a Kenneth."

"Who mentioned him?"

"Detective Batista."

"Oh yeah. He did say that was his first name," I said recalling his introduction. "Are you and he friends?"

He shrugged. "I guess you could say that. We're more than acquaintances. He was helping my brother, too."

Too, I thought. As if he was saying I was helping his brother.

"I didn't know your brother," I said for the third time. Seemed like I needed to pound that into everyone's head around here. "And I wasn't helping him or intending to help him. Kenneth is— was my fiancé." I shook that thought out of my head. "My boyfriend . . . Ugh . . . He is now and has been for a while, my *ex*-boyfriend."

"Where is Kenneth?"

"In Florida."

"He left Rio?"

"He was never here."

"How did you come here to meet your ex-boyfriend if he was never here?"

"I thought the note that your brother sent me was from Kenneth."

"Gerson signed the note, didn't he?"

"He signed it "G," I said. "I thought that stood for . . . Oh, never mind." I closed my eyes to collect my thoughts. "How did your brother say he knew me?" I asked. There had to be some logical explanation on this connection between the two of us.

"You met him at the airport when you were leaving for Rome." He looked at me. "You don't remember?"

"I remember that I *didn't* meet him."

"You told him your name. That you were going on vacation to Rome. Where you were staying. For how long. But, you said, that was only your cover story. Although you did plan on 'playing tourist'," he did the air quotes, "while you were there."

"My cover story?" I hiked up an eyebrow.

"Yes. You told him that you were a private investigator working in Tallahassee. You worked for several lawyers and that you were really good at what you do, and now that business was taking you to Rome."

"*I* told him that?" I pointed a finger at my chest.

"Yes. He asked if you could help him. You told him that you knew all about his case. And if you didn't have a plane to catch, you probably could tell him a few things that might help."

Pick up where we left off . . . That was what that meant, I thought.

"So all of this is about his case? The one where he 'allegedly' murdered someone?" I did the air quotes thingy back.

"Yes." He stopped walking and locked eyes with me. "So, you lied to my brother? You aren't really a private investigator with information about his case?"

"No."

"Then why did you say all of that?"

"No, I mean I didn't lie. I never met your brother." I stepped toward him, but he backed up, it seemed now he didn't want to be near me. I blew out a breath. "Did your brother tell you what I looked like?" I asked that because people always commented and described me by my red hair.

"No. Not really, other than you wore big glasses that kept falling off of your face."

Chapter Seven

"Oh! That four-eyed faker!" I stomped my foot and flung back my coconut as if I was getting ready to throw it. "I am going to choke her as soon as I get back home."

"What?" Enes said, a confused look on his face. He took the coconut out of my hand. "Who?"

"My travel agent," I said, screeching. "I'd bet a whole year's worth of milk money it was my travel agent your brother spoke to. My *ex*-travel agent. Oooh, I could just wring her neck!"

"I don't understand."

So I told him the story of loose-fitting-eyeglass-wearing-storyteller   Angie Sinclair Abbot and her fake identity machinations.

"So it was all a ruse?" he said, after listening to my explanation. He narrowed his eyes, seemingly trying to digest what I told him. "She just said she was you and made up the story about being a private eye?"

"Yeah. As far as I can see, that's what happened," I said. "What else could it be?" I threw up my hands. "She goes out to the airport a lot for her job. She probably just ran into him and started telling her lies."

"So my brother contacts you—thinking you were an investigator—sends a ticket for you to come here and you're dragged into all this murder stuff for nothing?" He held out his hands.

"It looks that way," I said. "Because I surely don't know anything. Thanks to Angie, it looks like I got a ticket to murder."

Nodding his head, he processed what I'd said. "I guess you did get a ticket to murder." He smacked his lips. "Well, that answers that," he said. He stood and looked at me for a moment, then walked over to a nearby trashcan and dumped our coconuts in it. He walked back over to me swiping his hands together. "You ready to go?" he asked.

I turned and looked back down the crescent coastline, people still soaking up what was left of the day's sun. I was still pretty upset with Angie, but there wasn't anything I could do about it at the moment. I looked back at Enes. Even if Angie dealt me a bad hand, I was at least enjoying his company.

"There are a couple of miles of beach left," he said, noticing my hesitation. "It never sleeps, always jumping. Always people here." He looked down at me. "But to be honest with you. I'm beat. I found my brother dead today and the only thing that was holding me together, and what I was waiting on before I called home to let our parents know, was that I thought you had information that could help clear his name. Make everything right. Give my parents some consolation. But you're just a kindergarten teacher."

I opened my mouth to speak.

He held up a hand to stop me. "I'm not saying anything is wrong with that, I'm just saying now I know you can't help me. And I just want to go home and cry."

I looked at him, my heart suddenly breaking for him. I realized just then, in the midst of everything, he had stayed cool and collected. Now, evidently because of me not being who he and his brother thought I was, he had nothing left. I could see how worn he was.

"We can go," I said, staring up into his eyes.

"Good," he said. "Because I can't handle much more. Not today."

I rubbed his arm, wanting to say something but not finding the words. He spoke instead. "And yes," he said, "grown men do cry."

I could see the heaviness that Enes carried, and wondered what I'd do if he started bawling like I had done back at the hotel.

On the walk back to the car he didn't seem to stand as tall as he had earlier. And he was quiet for most of the ride back, pensive, breaking the silence only after the ride was almost over.

"We'll be back there in a minute," he said, not explaining exactly where *there* was. "Your luggage is still at the bar where you left it before you went down to the station."

"I know," I said. I glanced over at him. "I need to find a place to stay, I guess. I don't know how long that detective is going to try to keep me here."

He looked over at me. "I'll see if I can't talk to him about that. Now that I've found out . . ." He blew out a breath, not finishing his sentence. He hit his hand on the steering wheel and let out a grunt. He put on the blinker and changed lanes, collecting himself it seemed before he spoke again. "We'll have to tell him that you don't know anything."

"You think that'll help. If you talk to him?"

"He's reasonable."

"Scary, is more like it," I said. "All nice to me at first, then he got dismissive. Shooing me away like I was a pesky little child," I said. "He could make things bad for me, I've heard about foreign policemen."

"And what have you heard?" he asked. His face seemed to lighten in amusement with my statement.

"How they throw you in jail for something as minor as shoplifting and then send you home in a body bag."

He chuckled. "This isn't North Korea," he said. "How did you go to Rome all by yourself if you're such a scared little Nelly?"

"I'm not scared, just informed," I said. "This government might protect your brother because he was a citizen, but I'm sure they'd just throw me to the wolves."

"I won't let them," he said. "I'll protect you. Keep that big bad Jorge away from you."

"Don't patronize me," I said.

"I'm not," he said. "I think once he understands what happened. How you got here on the wrong pretense, he'll let you go." He shrugged. "Maybe your boyfriend can come down?" He watched for my reaction out of the side of his eyes. "You know, so you don't feel all alone. Stay with you until you can get the okay to go home."

"I told you, he's my *ex*-boyfriend."

"I know. But you must still be on good terms," he said. "You came to Rio to see him. To be with him, didn't you?"

"Yes. But, I think subconsciously, I don't like him very much. So it's a good thing he wasn't here and that things are not going to work out between us."

"Subconsciously? Like on some other deeper level?" he asked.

"On all levels."

He laughed. "Why do you say that?"

"Because I just knew that was him on the floor in that hotel room. Dead."

"That's not bad to think. You thought you were coming here to meet him. Makes sense he'd be the one there."

"No. I thought it was him even after I saw your brother. I must have manifested," I swirled my hands up around my head, "or convinced myself mentally somehow that that was him on that floor," I said. "Like I wanted it to be him. I mean, I even told Detective Batista that I saw Kenneth on that floor dead. Practically argued the point."

"So . . ." he said and glanced over at me. "You must really have some bad feelings going on about that guy. Your ex-boyfriend."

I shook my head, my eyes glazing over. "Somewhere deep inside, I guess I do." I looked at Enes. "But that can't be good. I teach five-year-olds. I can't go around having psychotic thoughts buried deep inside of me. They can be little monsters at times." I frowned up. "I can't be secretly hiding that I'm a monster slayer that might snap one day."

He laughed. "I wouldn't worry about it. You feeling that way about Kenneth, who I'm guessing must have been far left from Mr. Right, won't have any bearing on the kids in your class."

"My mother told me I should stop watching the *ID Channel*. That I had some sort of fixation on it, and it had a hold on me. Messing with my brain."

"The what?"

"It's like a documentary-style television channel that tells the stories of true crime. Mostly homicides."

"Oh," he said, nodding that he understood. "The Manchurian Candidate, huh?"

I giggled. "Exactly. At least that what my mother says."

"Tell Mom, I agree." He shook his head, a lopsided grin on his face. "That just couldn't be good for you, watching shows about murder all the time."

"It doesn't make me feel safe anymore, that's for sure. About anything. Everywhere I go, I'm looking over my shoulder. I think murderers are just lurking in the shadows, waiting to get me."

"Then why do you keep watching them?"

I leaned back on the headrest. "I don't know," I said in a whiny voice. "I guess I'm addicted. I get home from school and I can't wait to turn the television on."

"That's pretty bad," he said. "You shouldn't do that to yourself."

I pushed his arm gently. "You're a lawyer, you must be inundated with it. And you made it your profession, so you must like it, too."

"Ouch," he said and rubbed his arm.

"That didn't hurt," I said.

"And no, I am not inundated with murder." He chuckled. "I do civil cases, bankruptcies, personal injury," he said. "If I worked in criminal law, I would've let my brother use my investigator. Not let him be conned by some dubious travel agent at the airport."

"Don't worry about her," I said. "I'll be taking care of her when I get back."

"Yeah, well just don't try any of those fail safe murder plots you've watched on TV. That's why I don't do criminal law, I don't know if I'm representing someone that's really guilty. And believe me, people eventually get caught."

"I know," I said. "Although, I can usually spot where they went wrong."

"Oh-ho-ho-ho," he said, chuckling. "And you think you could get away with it. You can commit the perfect crime? Not get caught?"

"Nope. They'd never know it was me."

"Be careful. Everyone thinks that," he said and then got quiet. His eyes turning intense, he got lost in thought.

"You okay?" I asked, sorry I said something that had dampened the mood. I was enjoying our conversation.

He looked at me and gave me a slight smile. "Yeah, just wondering if they'll find who killed my brother. His was so random." He bit his bottom lip. I didn't speak, waiting for him to finish his thought. It took him a moment or two to start to speak again. "Maybe," he said, "it's one of those where the killer doesn't get caught, you know?" He blinked and I thought I saw one of those "grown man tears" well up in his eye.

"You don't think they'll be able to find out who murdered him? Because without the police releasing information about how he died, it'll be easier to narrow in on someone, don't you think?"

"I don't know what to think. The only thing I know for sure is that crime—especially homicide, like I told you, is rampant in Rio." He shook his head seemingly disgusted. "So many random and senseless murders that I don't know if it's possible to determine who did this to my brother even with the police withholding pertinent information." He shrugged his shoulders. "Even with the homicide detective a friend." He tugged at his eye with his finger as if he had something in it. "And especially since my brother was wanted for murder."

"But that was in Florida," I said.

"The stigma associated with that disgusts people all over the world. Who wants to help a murderer?"

"You mean other than you and Detective Batista?"

That got a chuckle out of him. "Yeah, besides the two of us. But something like that might make people not want to help to find out what happened to him."

"What happened with the murder in Florida?"

He shook his head. "It's a long story. I don't even feel like talking about that." He looked at me and smiled. "And before you say, you've got nothing but time, we're here." He pulled up in front of the bar and pointed. "I'm going to get you settled. Tomorrow first thing, I'll go talk to Jorge. See what I can do to get you back home to your crime television obsession. I hate thinking how my brother got you caught up in a real one."

"My encounter with a real one is going to happen as soon as I get home."

"Oh yeah, your attempt at the perfect murder. First victim, Angie the travel agent," he said.

"Dead Angie, is what they'll be calling her." I formed my fingers like they were wrapped around her throat. "I might just end up on the *ID Channel* myself."

Chapter Eight

He walked out from behind a corner. A big, burly guy with a buzz haircut and a ruddy face. I was startled more so than frightened at him materializing in front of me. He sidestepped to get in front of Enes as we walked in the door of the Watering Hole. Enes had held the door for me and followed in behind me.

"It's not enough that you two kept trouble going up in the states." The words spewed out of the man's mouth, saliva collecting on his lips. "Now you wanna come here and try to do the same thing."

"What are you talking about?" Enes said. Enes tried to get around the guy, but the guy used his girth to trap Enes at the door. Enes stood tall and faced him.

My heart about stopped when I realized this guy was trying to put a beat down on Enes. I moved out of the way and headed toward the bar. Figured if I was close to it, I could grab a bottle if I needed to break it over Burly Guy's head.

"I never liked that little rat brother of yours, anyway," Burly Guy continued his row. "Then like a little chicken he runs down here to hide out when his true, inherited nature comes out."

"You don't know what you're talking about," Enes said. "Get out of my face." I could see the muscles in Enes' jaw tightened and his eyes had become fiery.

"Now Job!" The woman I'd seen behind the bar earlier ran over, leaving her customers to stop "Job" as she called him from pounding on Enes.

It was the first time I'd heard barkeep speak. She talked with a twang, one of the few accents I'd heard since I'd been in

Rio. With me being hooked on phonics, I wasn't sure if with her accent she wasn't mispronouncing "Job," the Biblical name with the long "o" and saying it so it sounded like the word j-o-b.

"None of this is called for." Her face was turning red trying to intervene. Then she spelled out her disapproval. "B-A-D," she said, like she was speaking to a child, then grabbed Burly Guy's arm. She pushed her body up against his but it was like an ant trying to move a mountain. Even with all the force she mustered up from her anger, it was easy to see that her small frame was no match for his. With a push of his arm, he swatted at her as if she were an annoying mosquito.

"Go on, Rose, this ain't your fight." His voice boomed through the small barroom, echoing throughout.

"It shouldn't be a fight at all," Rose answered back. "Those boys have never done anything to you." She stood between him and Enes. "And one of 'em is dead. Show some respect."

"Rose, I can handle him," Enes said, then turned to Burly Guy. "Go ahead. Do what you want to do!" Enes wasn't backing down even though Burly Guy was twice his size.

"No!" Rose screeched. "B-A-D!" she said turning to Enes she smacked him on the chest. Then she turned to face Burly Guy and repeated her action, spelling out her description of him as well. "B-A-D!"

"Mickey," Enes called out without taking his eyes off Burly Guy. "Come get your mother. I think Job needs to get something off his chest."

Now Enes was calling him job . . .

A thin, younger man, perhaps in his thirties, popped up out of his seat at the bar and scuttled over. "C'mon, Ma. Let Enes handle this." He pulled on her arm, but she was reluctant to leave. He had to get on the other side of her and push her back out of the way.

"I'm going to put something on you," Job said. He balled up his fist and clenched his jaw.

"Have at!" Enes said. "See if you can. But I'd be real careful if I were you because you'll be sorry if I have to handle this."

"Neither one of you don't need to try and handle anything," Rose called over as her son was pushing her away.

"Enes can't handle anything," Job said. "And I got something for him that'll stop him cold. Just like his brother." He stepped closer to Enes now that Rose had been moved out of the way. "You a lawyer," Job continued, "your brother a doctor and you're still both scum. Just can't take the bad out of people. Only one way to fix problems like the two of you." He was spitting his angry words out. "And that's to get rid of you. For good. Gerson was taken care of, now all that's left is you."

"Don't talk about my brother," Enes said, a guttural sound emanated from his throat. At first I thought it was going to be some kind of war cry, but he just laughed. "And you don't scare me." This time Enes shortened the distance between them. They were practically nose-to-nose. "You don't want to mess with the kind of bad I got in me."

Rose broke away from her son and came scurrying back over to try again to get between the two warring factions. Mickey, her son, came scrambling behind her, trying to catch her. He couldn't get her to back down.

"Enes, please," Rose said, arriving back to where they stood and squeezing between them.

"He started it, Rose," Enes said, holding up both his hands and taking a step back. "I'm just making sure it's ended once and for all."

"I will call your *mamãe*," Rose said to Enes. "I swear I will. I know you haven't told her about Gerson and it would break her heart to know both her boy got into trouble on the same day."

Enes took another menacing look at Job.

"C'mon, give me what you got," Job said, gesturing with his hands urging Enes to have a go at him.

"We can finish this later," Enes said, his eyes on Job. Then he looked down at Rose and back at Job, the anger leaving his eyes. "I'm going to respect her and her establishment, and you are too."

"I don't want your respect," Rose said turning to Job. "After this, I don't even want to see you in my bar. Ever again."

"You siding with this guy?" Job tried to jab Enes with his finger, but Enes pushed it out of the way. "That's how his brother ended up like he did, trying to get away with stuff."

"What are you talking about?" Enes asked. Seemingly ready to start up again, after his ire, I thought, had been squelched.

"He ain't talking about nothing. As usual." Short Rose bent her neck back to look up at Job. "It's time for you to go."

"Fine," he said. "This isn't the only place I can take care of that no good bottom feeder." And with that he marched out of the door.

After Job left, Enes started pacing the floor. "What the heck was he talking about?" he asked to no one in particular.

I sat down on the stool by where I'd been standing. I'd been tense the entire time, and now with Job gone, all I could do was try to catch my breath.

"He wasn't talking about anything," Rose said, she was following behind Enes, step-for-step. "Leastways nothing to get yourself riled up about."

Enes went across the width of the bar a few times before he worked his way over to stand near it. He turned and faced Rose who practically bumped into him. "He was talking like he knew something," Enes said.

"Something like what?" she asked.

"Like who killed Gerson," he said.

"No." She shook her head and pulled her over-sized sweater closed. "He doesn't know anything."

"Maybe . . ." Enes tilted his head and bit his bottom lip. "Maybe he might have been the one who did it."

Rose didn't respond to him. She drew in a breath and put a shaky hand up to her head brushing strands of thin hair from her face. "I've got to tend to the bar," she muttered more to herself than to anyone and walked away from him. "Been enough commotion in here today. Too much. Patrons'll be flocking out the door."

Enes looked over at me, and nodded his head vigorously. "We need to find out what he was doing at the time my brother was murdered." He gave a final resolute nod. "I think we may have just come up with our first murder suspect."

Did he say "we" . . .

Chapter Nine

Enes must not have noted how I retreated to the bar during the little melee in order to get out of the way. Maybe he needed to be reminded how scary he had determined I was.

Rose, on the other hand, was a feisty little woman. She stood right there in between them. He could probably count on her for help.

So, with me being a scared little Nelly, as he had put it earlier, I didn't know what Enes was thinking when he said "we" had to look into Job's whereabouts at the time Gerson was killed. I was just counting down the minutes until I could go home.

I looked over at Enes, sparks from the flame of his anger still flickering. I decided not to appear to be the wimp I truly was, especially after the way Enes stood up to the bully, Job. So I pretended I was standing there to get my suitcase.

"Is my luggage still behind the bar?" I asked Mickey who, after giving up on trying to get his mother roosted, had ambled back to his barstool.

Even though at the moment I was using it as my alibi, I still was worried about my suitcase and could only hope that it hadn't come up missing. I'd left abruptly, not asking anyone in particular to watch it. I wasn't sure how Enid was feeling about me since I'd lied to her about my name. And then with everyone telling me how bad Rio was, and witnessing (okay, nearly witnessing) my first barroom brawl ever, I had started to feel fearful of the entire city.

I was sorry about feeling that way about Rio, though, because everything

I'd seen in the city was beautiful. The weather was breezy and calm, the vistas stunning, and I had to admit, I enjoyed the company of Enes Crawford.

"Oh, yeah. Your luggage is still there," Mickey said and gave me a sideways grin. "Safe and sound. You want me to get it?"

"Here, give this to Enes." I looked up and it was Rose. She'd given me a tall glass filled with ice and a clear liquid. I didn't detect an odor, so I assumed it was water. I'd think, as a bartender, she'd see that he needed something a little stronger.

I took it. "You think it'll help?"

"You got something better?"

I didn't, so I walked over to him. He had landed in a booth and was sitting there, his hands placed on the table and his eyes fixed on them. I pushed the glass of water toward him, but he didn't take it. "Rose sent this over. She said it might help."

Not reaching for the glass, he looked up at me. "Sorry," he said. "Bad thing to air out dirty laundry in front of company."

"It's okay," I said. He finally reached out and took the water from me. "What was that all about?" I asked as I scooted into the bench opposite him.

"Long story."

"You have a few of those, don't you?"

He looked at me puzzled then realized that that had been what he'd told me about his brother's involvement in the murder back in Florida.

"Yeah, I do," he said. "That's why I don't like coming down here. There's always some kind of drama."

"You mean to Rio?"

"Yes," he said and huffed. "I stay in Florida. I only came this time to help my brother." He glanced over at me. "I had just arrived when . . . I found him. It had told me to meet him in that room. I guess in anticipation of you arriving."

"Is that where you were going when I saw you?"

"No," he frowned up. "You know by then it had already happened. I had found him before that. Just before that. I had to step out. I didn't want to mess up the crime scene. I didn't want to look at him lying there. I didn't want anyone to hear me talking to the police. I closed the door and went to the lobby to report what I'd found."

"Oh," I said. "Why were you going back up there?"

"To stand guard. I didn't know if the murderer would come back, or if housekeeping would try to get it."

"How did you know where I'd gone?" I asked.

"I watched from the hotel window. I started to chase after you, I figured you must be Rowan, but I needed to stay with him."

"Even without the glasses you thought I was the person your brother was expecting."

"Contacts. I figured you had on contacts."

"You stayed really calm and thought rationally," I said. "In the same circumstances, I don't know that I could have done that."

"I had come here to help him, so I was helping him the best way I could. It was the least that I could do. Now," Enes hung his head, "I'm ending up having to bury him. And I hadn't ever thought, until Job made that statement, that perhaps it's somebody we know who killed him."

"Your brother had enemies?" Not wanting to speak ill of the dead, I flinched as the words tumbled out of my mouth.

He didn't immediately say anything. I saw his jaw working like he was chewing on something. He hadn't even put the glass to his mouth yet, so I knew it wasn't a piece of ice—he was thinking. I'd seen him do that earlier.

He did a *rat-a-tat-tat* on the table, drumming his hands and popped up out of his seat. "We need to get you squared away," he said. Evidently, he'd had enough of the murder conversation. He walked over to the counter and set the glass down. "Rose," he said, getting her attention away from her customer, "I want to get a room for Rowan upstairs. Can you put her up?"

When I heard his question to her, I scrambled out of my seat and sidled up next to him.

"Rowan, huh?" Rose said. She came over to where we were standing. "I don't think I ever was properly introduced."

"Rose this is Rowan." He looked over at me and smiled. "She's a friend of the family back in Florida. She was registered to stay in the room where . . ." He lowered his eyes and took a measured breath. "You know."

"Enes," I tugged at his shirt. He hadn't discussed this with me, and I wasn't sure I wanted to stay over a bar where people came in wanting to fight. "I can just get another hotel room."

"Where?" he asked and raised an eyebrow.

He knew I didn't know of anywhere.

"It's better you stay here," he said. "I'm staying here, and I can keep an eye on you."

Keep an eye on me? Why didn't you just say that in the first place, I thought. I had to keep myself from batting my eyelashes.

"Okay," I said, acting reluctant. "If there's room." I looked at Rose sheepishly, secretly crossing my fingers behind my back.

"Of course I've got room." She opened up the cash register and took out a key. Handing it to Enes she said, "Give her the room across the hall from you. I'll bring up some fresh towels in a few minutes."

I followed him through the bar, down a short hallway, past the kitchen and up two short flights of steps. The upstairs hall was carpeted, the walls freshly painted and a table sat along the wall with a vase of flowers. There looked to be about six or seven rooms down the hallway.

"I hope you don't mind," Enes said unlocking the door and swinging it open for me, "but I need to get to my room so I can call my parents." He pointed across the hall. "They still don't know about

Gerson. I'm dreading that conversation." He pulled his cell phone out of his pants pocket and checked the time. "There's only an hour's difference between there and here, so I want to call before they go to bed."

"No problem," I said trying to sound chipper. "I'm good."

"You'll be okay?" he asked even though I'd just said I would be.

"Yes," I said with a smile. I peeked my head in the door to the room and took a gander around it. The room was a fairly good size. Everything, though, was brown. The bed, the curtains (at least they were sheer), the carpet, the dresser. Ah, there was a pink throw pillow. I guess that was there for a "pop" of color. I could see an ensuite bathroom. Good, I thought, I don't have to share with whoever else was renting a room from her.

Turning my head back to him, I nodded in approval. "I know you're tired and I know it'll be hard to talk to your parents." I tried to give him a smile that didn't betray how much I'd enjoyed spending the day with him and how sorry I was it was coming to an end. "And you should try to get some rest."

"I don't think that's going to happen," he said, handing me the key to my room. "Looks like I might start practicing criminal law tonight. I need to find out where Job was this afternoon and if he knew anything."

"How do you plan on doing that?" I asked

"Not sure," he said. "I guess just ask around."

"Well, if you need me to help, I'll do whatever I can."

Did I just say that?

"And don't worry about me," I said, continuing to talk out of character. "I'll be fine." I reassured him.

But I knew that wasn't the truth and the gravity of it hit me as soon as I stepped inside the room and closed the door.

What in the world was I doing?

I plopped down on the bed and looked around me. I was nervous. Afraid of everything going on around me. The murder. Possible murderers right in the same room with me. Being held hostage by the police in a foreign country. Him calling me Scared Nelly was right.

I put my hand over my chest and could feel my heart thumping. I licked my lips and closed my eyes.

But on top of all that, I was feeling some type of way about Enes.

"OMG!"

I didn't know what to do about anything.

Should I just go to bed as if this hadn't been the freakiest day of my life and sleep?

"No!" I popped up. I couldn't do that. I started pacing the floor.

But what was it I was supposed to do?

I knew one thing for sure. I was not supposed to be in this kind of predicament. A real life *ID Channel* drama. Who would have thought it?

What was I thinking when I hopped onto that plane? All I had to do was call Kenneth, like I did at the police station, find out he hadn't sent for me and I wouldn't be in the middle of all this mess. But no.

Then you wouldn't have met Enes . . .

The thought of that made me smile.

I turned and looked at myself in the mirror. My light skin covered with freckles, my thick red hair frizzed from the humidity. I had on the same clothes I'd worn on the plane, that I crawled around in in the bloody room, and when I was shackled to the chair in the police station. Okay, so I wasn't exactly shackled. Not even handcuffed. But still . . .

I tried to run my fingers through my hair, but they wouldn't get through it. I tried to brush over my clothes, but they were not even close to presentable. I had to laugh.

I hadn't looked in a mirror all day, and that turned out to be a good thing.

No way I'd impressed a man with my looks. Not today.

Was I trying to impress Enes?

I felt a blush coming on.

Is that possible? I thought. Am I attracted to Enes? I stared at my reflection. Aren't I still in love with Kenneth?

The one that you subconsciously wished were lying on that hotel room floor dead?

Oh yeah. I forgot about that.

I sat on the bed. Folded my hands in my lap, and taking in calming breaths, I tried to understand what I was feeling. It was just like I told the children in my class to do. I'd say, "Now you just sit there and think about that."

But now I understood the blank looks on their faces when I put them there. I didn't know what to think.

Not only did I like Enes, I wanted to help him find the killer, or do whatever it took to make him happy. Yes. That's it! I wanted to help. I mean, technically, it was what I had come down to Rio to do. I just didn't know how I could go about that.

A *tap tap* on the door broke my train of thought.

"Come in," I said. I sat up nice and straight and put a small smile on my face. I wanted to look pleasant, but not anxious when Enes opened the door, even though my heart pounding told the story about how happy it made me. Only it was Rose who entered, not Enes. "Hi." I didn't want to seem disappointed.

"It's just me," she said. "Came to bring you the towels."

"Thank you," I said. "I hope you take credit cards." I reached for my purse. "I haven't had the time to exchange any currency."

"I take American money. I'm American, you know."

"I know," I said.

"But you don't worry none about that," she said. "Everything's taken care of for you."

I sat even more straight and smiled. "Enes?" I asked. Then, I thought, I didn't want to give away how that made me feel. "Because he needn't do that. I can take care of it myself."

"Like I said, already taken care of. After what you've been through today, I think it's only fair he do it."

"Thank you," I said. "I really appreciate that."

"No problem," Rose said. "Now, rules for the house. Did Enes tell you?"

"No," I said. Eyes wide, ready to learn, like my kindergarten students, I listened for her instructions.

"First, you keep your own room clean. If you want the bed made up, you make it. I don't much care, but I don't want it looking like a tornado hit the place. Mickey comes in once a week and cleans the bathrooms, dusts and vacuums. I used to do it, but I just can't do it anymore. Running the bar is enough. You're responsible for your own things, so make sure you lock your door. No disturbing the other guests. Right now you and Enes are my only two here, but still as you can tell, I don't like trouble. And two . . ."

Hadn't she named more than one thing already?

"There's a kitchen downstairs," she continued. "Probably saw it when Enes brought you up. I cook breakfast. Not to order. I serve it at eight. If you miss it, you're on your own. I can be late, you can't," she warned. "Other than that I keep cold cuts, bread, fruit, that sort of thing. You can make yourself a sandwich. I used to cook food at the bar, but not anymore. So the rest of the day you're on your own."

"Yes ma'am. I got it," I said.

Rose laid the towels on the dresser and had started to walk out when I decided I should try and get some information out of her. After all, I had decided to help Enes.

"You mind if I ask you what all that was about downstairs," I said.

"Say what?" She turned back toward me, squinting her eyes. She cupped a hand behind her ear as if she was trying to rein in the sound waves, direct them through her little funnel. "I'm a little hard of hearing these days." She shook her head. "They used to play that music so loud down in the bar I think it made me deaf. I had to get rid of that jukebox."

"Oh, okay," I said and chuckled.

"If I'm not facing you," she said, "where I can see your lips, just talk loud. I won't think you're rude."

"I was just asking . . ." I tried not to make my voice too loud, I didn't want Enes across the hall hearing me being nosy. I peeked around Rose to see if his door was shut, but I couldn't tell. "I was just wondering what that was about downstairs. You know, with the other guy and Enes."

"I didn't like what happened down there one bit," she said. She pushed the door out of her way and came back in the room. "And as one of my guests, I'm sorry you had to witness that. Those kind of things don't usually happen here. I don't know what got into Job." She dipped her head. "Well, I do, but he should know better."

"Is his name Job, like a job you work?"

"Yes. That ain't his real name, though. His name is Clinton Maylock, but we call him Job because he is a piece of work."

I chuckled. "I could see that."

"He don't like them Crawford boys not one little bit." She shook her head. "It's a grudge he'd been holding a long time."

"Why doesn't he like them?" I couldn't see why anyone wouldn't like Enes. He was smart. Handsome. And he didn't back down from a fight, something I found appealing.

"Oh," she waved her hand. "That goes back a long time." She went and sat in the side chair and leaned toward me. I shifted around so I could look at her. "Job's brother was in love with a girl named Emilie. Beautiful girl."

"She was from Brazil?" I asked.

"Huh?" She blinked her eyes a few times. "Yeah, Yeah. She was. And so was

Job's brother. They've got different fathers. Job's father is an American, raised him up there in Connecticut. Now listen."

"Okay," I said, letting her tell the story without interrupting.

"Now his brother, Carlos, they called him Chewy-"

I wanted to ask about that name, but thought better of it.

"Chewy was a lot older than Job, ten or twelve years older," she was saying, "so Job really looked up to him. Thought the world of him. And since Chewy thought he was gonna marry Emilie, always bragged he would, that made Job keen on her, too. Now Chewy had had his eyes set on Emilie for as long as anyone could remember and even when she came up pregnant by another guy, he still was steadfast in his love."

"Wow, that's true love."

"Sure it is," she said. "But most times that kind of love is crazy love. Don't do nobody no good."

"She didn't end up with Chewy?"

"Who?" She frowned up. "What'd you say?"

"You said it was a crazy love, I was just wondering did Chewy and Emilie end up together."

Her eyes got big. "Hold on, I'ma tell you." She shook her head. "Now then, both Chewy and Emilie were from a favela." She nodded and pointed at me. "You know what that is?"

"No," I said.

"It's the Brazilian slum. Like the projects back in the states."

I knew about that. Although I grew up and lived in a small town where everyone was middle class, I worked in the inner-city neighborhoods of Tallahassee. A lot of my students lived in projects.

"Oh," I said nodding that I understood.

"So, the boy that got Emilie pregnant had come down here to stay a few months," Rose continued. "He wasn't from no projects, if you know what I mean."

I nodded.

"Emilie didn't have to think twice about dating a boy from the United States. Heck, she figured he could have been her ticket out. Now, that boy's name was Joseph. He was a college student and down here for a semester learning class. I forget what they're called."

"A semester abroad?"

"Yeah," she wiggled her fingers at me, "something like that." She swallowed, readying to tell the rest of her story. "He stayed in the room right across the hall that summer. The same one Enes is in." She leaned forward and peeked out the door, as if she was checking on Enes.

"Yep. Enes always gets that room when he comes," she continued. "So—getting back to the story—the two of them, Emilie and Joseph got along real well. Two peas in a pod, and they fell in love. But then it came time for him to go back home. To the states. He told her he'd come back to see her, but no one believed that."

"Did he ever come back?" I asked.

"I'm getting to that if you let me tell the story."

I nodded my okay.

"When he left, he didn't know she was pregnant. She didn't tell him. I'm not sure if she knew at the time. After a while she gave birth and tried to do the best she could by herself to raise her baby."

"That can be hard," I said. I slipped up and interrupted her again, but I'd thought about some of the kids that lived where I taught school. I could sympathize with what she was saying.

"Did you say 'hard?' I tell you I can hardly hear up here," Rose said, leaning in closer and turning her ear to me. "The bar echoes so I can hear better down there. And you got such a soft voice."

I had been using my inside voice not wanting Enes to hear me snooping for information about him. "Yes, I said 'hard,'" I responded switching to my "outside for recess" voice.

"That's better," she said. "Yes, it was hard for her. I hated seeing her struggle. She was, still is, very beautiful."

"What happened?" I let the words out before I thought about it. "Sorry," I said.

"Well Chewy saw that as his opportunity. He convinced her Joseph wasn't coming back. No American doctor wanted a favela girl."

"Joseph was a doctor?" I frowned, hadn't she just said he was in school?

"Well, not when he came down here. He was in school." She looked at me. "I told you that part."

"Oh, right," I said. "Go ahead."

"And Emilie believed that Chewy might just be right. So she started letting him help her. You know. Give her money for food or if the boy needed something. And he'd practically got her down the aisle when Joseph showed back up."

I smiled. I felt like clapping my hands in glee. I wanted her to end up with Joseph and I'm such a sucker for happy endings. "Joseph came back for her? For Emilie?"

"Why else would he come back?" she said. "He didn't know until he got here that she had had his child. And he might have only visited with her if it wasn't for the baby and left again. But as soon as he saw that boy, he married Emilie and took them both back to the states."

"Ah, so Chewy was mad."

"He went crazy. Literally. It broke his heart so bad, he went off the deep end. Started drinking, ending up killing a woman. It was an accident, but she was dead nonetheless."

"Oh my! Is he in jail?"

She shook her head. "Not anymore. But he is a wasted man. Job takes care of him."

"So what does that have to do with Enes?"

"That baby was Gerson."

"Oh!" My eyes got big. "Emilie and Joseph are Enes' parents?" I remembered that Enes told me that Gerson had been born in Brazil.

"Yep," Rose said, nodding. "And Job blames all of them, not just Joseph, for his brother's downfall." She stood up. "And as you can see, it's affected him, too."

"Yeah, I see," I said. I went and stood by the door, checking to make sure Enes was still inside his room. "So do you think that maybe Job could have been the one who killed Gerson?"

"It's possible," she said. "Sure sounded like he was insinuating that today. But personally, I don't think so. He's just all bark. Plus, there are a lot of people around here that would have wanted to pop Gerson upside his head and split open his skull."

She flipped her hand like she was coming down on his head with some kind of object she was holding. "*Bam*," she said.

Chapter Ten

"Oh my!" I said after she left and closed the door behind her. "Rose knows how Gerson was killed. Wasn't that supposed to be a secret?"

What did that mean?

It means that she's a suspect.

That's exactly what it meant.

And don't forget about Job . . .

Job, I thought. Enes thought he might have something to do with it. Job, what a crazy name, albeit it's a nickname. That name was too hard for me. I kept wanting to call him the Biblical Job. I'll just call him by his given name—Clinton. I never let the kids in my class go by nicknames, I'll have to stick to my usual rules if I'm going to solve this murder.

Solve the murder . . .

I liked the sound of that. I could do it, I thought. Heck, I not only would figure out what the murderers on my favorite TV murder mystery shows had done wrong to get caught, I was usually able to figure out whodunit way before they announced it.

I had made up my mind to help Enes before Rose appeared with the towels, mostly because I had started liking him. But now after Rose's outburst of secret information, I had determined it was also the right thing to do. I was stuck here anyway.

So, if I wanted to help Enes, I needed to think about the murder logically.

"I need to write all of this down," I said aloud. "Make a list."

I checked the desk, and there was a small pad of paper and pen inside the desk drawer. I grabbed it and scooted onto the bed. I put my back up against the headboard and bent my knees so I could use my thighs as a flat surface ready to write.

I put "Murder Suspects" at the top. Then I wrote "Rose."

"Wait," I said. "I don't even know Rose's last name." So I moved on to the next line and wrote in "Clinton 'Job' Maylock."

Comes in handy being able to remember names. A talent I acquired from being a schoolteacher. And kindergarten teachers always used first and last names.

But then I didn't know what else to write.

Let, me think . . . I tapped the pen on my forehead.

But as hard as I thought, I couldn't think of anything else to write. I laid the notepad and pen on the nightstand next to the desk and got up.

Maybe if I busied myself, not concentrate on thinking, I could come up with something.

I grabbed my suitcase and lugged it up onto the bed. I unzipped it and unpacked my clothes. Happy I had taken the time to fold them, I didn't see an iron anywhere, I placed them in the drawers of the dresser.

I took my toiletry bag out and walked with it into the ensuite bathroom. I pulled out my toothbrush and toothpaste and laid them on the counter.

"First," I said to my reflection in the bathroom mirror, "I need to figure out who had the means, motive, and opportunity to commit the crime."

I smiled at my reflection. Yes! That's what I needed to do. "That's what the detectives on my shows always did first." By not concentrating, my mind had naturally started to put things in order.

I was a natural at this!

Okay, now how do I find out who had the means, motive and opportunity to kill Gerson Crawford?

I lined the tube of facewash and all of my 3 oz bottles filled with moisturizer, lotion and shampoo up on the vanity.

They would interview people. I glanced in the mirror and smiled at myself.

I can do that. I tilted my head and thought about it. I determined I had already interviewed both of them. Sort of. Clinton inadvertently. Without anyone asking him a word about it, he'd blabbed out enough to make himself suspicious.

I went back to the bed, sat down and picked up the notebook. I drew an arrow from Clinton's name and wrote in: A long, deep seated hatred for victim.

I nodded my head. Those were probably the exact words they'd use on *Fatal Attraction*.

Next I wrote "big guy." He was big enough to inflict bodily harm (a legal term I picked up from television detectives). And Gerson had died from blunt force trauma (another term I'd learned) I was sure of that. I knew that from the gash in the back of his head.

I put the notepad down and let my eyes drift off.

What had I seen?

I remember there was blood on the walls. I bit my lip. What else? That bloody rag.

What was that about? Had someone used it to wipe the blood from their hands? Because if they had, then their DNA would be on it.

But would a murderer just a throw evidence around like that?

We could analyze the towel. Well, *I* couldn't.

I'm sure they were doing that anyway.

But then I thought, maybe Gerson didn't die right away. Maybe the blood was on the wall and the towel because he used it to try and stop the bleeding . . .

But that was a pretty big gash I saw. Would someone be able to walk around and have the ability to try and treat himself with his skull bashed in like that?

He *was* a doctor . . .

Maybe the gash wasn't that big. I tried to remember it. I made a circle by cupping my hands and put them together. Then I stretched out my arms and squinted, trying to eyeball the size of the hole.

I flapped my hands down. I just wasn't sure I could count on what I saw. I mean, I saw Kenneth laying there and that wasn't right. I'd heard on television how eyewitness testimony can be faulty. Now I can see why.

And then there was Rose. I looked back at the paper I'd been writing on. There was nothing by her name. I didn't know if Clinton had the opportunity, not yet, but he had the means and the motive.

What was Rose's motivation? It was such an off-handed comment she made.

Plenty of people, she had said, *would want to split open his skull . . .*

Was she one of those people?

She also was small. I wasn't sure how tall Gerson was, or if he was muscular, but going by the way his brother looked, it was easy to imagine he was. Would Rose be able to take Gerson on?

What if she took him by surprise?

That would work. If she took him by surprise. The killing blow, from what I could tell came from the back. She could have came upon him unaware. Maybe he trusted her and didn't think twice about turning his back on her.

I wonder what the murder weapon was . . .

I chewed on my bottom lip and tried to visualize the room again. Had I seen the murder weapon? Was it sitting right there and in my panic missed it?

I let out a sigh.

There was more to this than I thought. I just didn't have enough information.

"I'm going to bed." I put the notepad and pen back on the desk and found a pair of shorts and T-shirt to put on to sleep in.

Then I heard my stomach rumbling.

I realized I hadn't had much to eat. So much had happened since the morning started with me getting that strange envelope. I was on a entirely different continent. And pining over an entirely different man.

I realized I was starving.

What *did* I eat today?

I remembered I had food on the plane. I didn't like it much, and then I had grabbed a sandwich at the airport after arriving in Rio. It had just been something light. I hadn't wanted my stomach growling when I saw Kenneth, but I hadn't wanted to be too full in case he wanted to take me out to lunch.

Gee, that had been so long ago . . .

Maybe I'll go and make me a sandwich, I thought. Rose had said I could. She said she kept "cold cuts." That had to mean lunchmeat. I'll just go down and grab something.

I slipped into my shorts and t-shirt and slid my feet back into my sandals. I grabbed the room key and gently shut the door. I couldn't see a light under Enes' door.

Maybe he's finish speaking with his parents and went to bed.

His day had been much worse than mine. I knew he must be dog tired.

But as I went down the stairs heading for the kitchen, I stopped in my tracks. I could smell him—his cologne and hear him talking low, but he must have had his phone on speaker because I could hear the person on the other end.

"I'm so glad you're coming," he said.

"You know I wouldn't let you go through this alone, Eric. I'm always there for you."

Eric?

Why was she calling him Eric, and who was "she?"

"I didn't think it would get this complicated," he said.

"I can do complicated," she said. "I'll be there for you just as soon as I can get a flight."

I didn't want to hear anymore. I ran back upstairs.

I was so foolish. Running here to see Kenneth after he'd made it clear he didn't want to see me anymore. I knew he didn't send me that note. I should have known or at least stopped and checked. And, now here I was doing it all over again. Falling for a guy. Readying to go around snooping to help him find a murderer for his brother when he had someone flying in that did complicated.

What did that even mean?

I didn't need him to make arrangements for me to go home. I was going to see to that myself and get the first flight home before things got too complicated for me.

Chapter Eleven

I tossed and turned all night. I was so confused. I had been so happy about the prospect of helping Enes with solving his brother's murder. Thinking that all my time spent watching true crime was going to be of some use.

And realizing, I didn't really want to go home.

I was in Rio de Janeiro. It had been fun going to the beach the day before, and not just because I had been with Enes. It was new and it was different. My entire visit so far had been filled with intrigue. That was something you didn't get from teaching kindergarten in Tallahassee, Florida. I wanted to see more of the city. The culture. Enes.

And that was the dilemma. I didn't know anything about being careful when it came to "more." I seemed to move forward blindly. Like hopping on a flight to see a man who hadn't given me a second thought after he had gave me the boot.

I woke early, the first sunlight streaming through the sheer curtained window seemed to smile at me.

My stomach was growling and I knew I'd better feed it. I had already let Ms. Complicated Solver keep me from getting a bite to eat. Rose told me breakfast was at eight. I picked up my phone. Six-thirty.

Wow, I thought. It was exactly twenty-four hours before that that I had gotten that envelope. The one that had sent me halfway across the world to a mystery that I didn't ever think possible in my boring life.

I hailed from Midspring, Florida. A little town on the fringe of Tallahassee that had blocks of tree-lined streets filled with neat little bungalows and manicured lawns. There were less than one thousand people and nearly all of them were related somehow. My family was one of the few black families that lived there, but we never had any problems.

Then after college, teaching school in the inner city of Tallahassee had been the big adventure for me. Tenement buildings, children counting on school lunches as the only sure meal they'd have for the day and having to dodge bullets at night instead of being able to do homework.

Me trying to understand their lives I think was what made me start watching true crime stories. One of my students had seen a show where he knew the people involved. How could a five-year-old know about that? I decided to find out about it myself, and just like the drugs they sell of the street corners of neighborhoods like those where I work, I was hooked.

I decided to call my mother. She hadn't the faintest idea what I'd gotten myself into. She thought I was still in Rome.

I remembered that Enes said there was only an hour's difference in Rio's time and Florida's. My mother "got up with the chickens," as they say. I didn't worry about waking her.

"Hi Mom," I said when she picked up. She didn't sound the least bit groggy.

"Morning!" she said cheerfully. "So good to hear your voice. Honey, it's Rowan." She was trying to wake my father. I could hear him groaning in the background. "Are you on your way home? What day is this?"

"Not sure when I'm coming home," I said.

"How is that?" she asked. "Don't you have a set itinerary?"

"I do—did, but something has come up."

"Oh no! Don't tell me you got into some kind of trouble. George wake up, Rowan's in trouble."

My parents had been married for nearly forty years, I was born second to the last of their four children. The only one doing something with their college degree they graciously paid for. Steady job or not, it seemed like they worried more about me than anyone else.

"I'm not in trouble, Mom. Don't wake Daddy," I said.

"I'm already woke," he said in the background. She must have put me on speakerphone.

"Well go back to sleep. I'm not in trouble, I'm just in Rio."

"Rio!" they said in unison.

"Rio de Janeiro?" My mother said.

"In South America?" my father asked. "Aren't you on the wrong continent?"

"Yes. Rio de Janeiro. I got an invitation to come here."

"From whom?" my father said.

"And you went," my mother said. "Oh Lord. Haven't you listened to anything we ever taught you?"

I didn't know specifically what she was talking about, because I couldn't remember her ever saying anything about not going to Rio . . .

"Are you okay?" my mother asked. "Do you want your father to come and get you?"

I chuckled. My thoughts exactly when I was sitting in that police station being interrogated by Detective Batista. Okay, so he didn't exactly interrogate me.

"No. I'm coming home soon. I have to get clearance from the homicide detective first."

"Oh Lord," my mother said, her voice going almost inaudible. I hope she hadn't fainted.

"Have you killed someone?" my father asked. I could hear in his voice he'd gotten up. I could just picture him putting on his pants, grabbing his wallet and keys to come and rescue me.

"She's killing me," my mother said, her voice muffled. She'd probably fallen back on the bed.

"No. I haven't killed anyone. It's a long story," I said, then smiled at the words. They were Enes' words. "But I'm okay, and I'll be back in Florida as soon as I can."

"When did you get there?" my mother asked. She seemed somewhat resuscitated.

"Yesterday," I said. "Early afternoon. So I really haven't been here that long."

"That long?" she said. She used the same words I had, but they had a completely different meaning.

"Who's there with you?" my father said.

"Uh . . . Enes," I said.

"Who is Enes?" Again, they said the words at the same time. Forty years of marriage had practically merged their brains.

"He's a lawyer. From Florida," I said. "I'm helping him work a case."

"I knew watching those television shows was going to get you in trouble," she said to me. The next questions she directed to my father. "Didn't I tell you, George that she had some glitch in her brain because of them?"

"Yep, you did," he said. "But I think she'll be okay."

My father had a way of placating my mother when she was reading me the riot act, but not really taking sides against me.

"I have to go," I said. "They're going to serve breakfast soon and I don't want to miss it."

"Who's going to be serving breakfast soon?" my mother said. "Are you going to at least tell us what hotel you're staying in?"

I realized I didn't know exactly where I was. Other than in Rio, I didn't know the name of the street or anything. When I arrived, I had just told the cab driver to take me to Casa Nova Hotel and I wasn't even there anymore. I was going to have to rectify that. Meanwhile, I needed to placate my parents.

"You'll be able to track me and get my address on your phone, Mom. Dad, you remember how to do it?"

I started a tracker program at our school. It caught on and was instituted in all the area grade and middle schools in the district. I called it KidProof.

I noticed even if my students complained of being hungry, or not having appropriate clothes to wear, their parents had cell phones and lots of times so did they. And more times than not, they had iPhones. And for those families that didn't have a phone for parent and child, we raised money to get trackable bracelets. Plastic bracelets, for some reason, were pretty popular and we had no trouble getting the kids to wear them.

Faculty and staff helped to educate parents on how to track their children. I decided to teach my parents as well. None of their children were minors, but they had an itch to always want to know where we were.

I think I was the only one of my siblings that had actually let them intrude that deeply into their lives.

"Yeah, I remember how to do it," my dad said. "Just don't make your mother worry about you too much." I knew he included himself in that warning.

"I won't," I said.

"How will I know when you're home?" my mother asked, her voice wavering in and out.

"Just keep your eye on the red dot," I said.

Chapter Twelve

I showered, humming happily along to a favorite Bruno Mars song and careful not to wet my hair too much. I dried off, tried to press down some of the pouf in my natural red doo and got dressed.

I wanted to get downstairs and eat breakfast, surely, but more than that, I wanted to see Enes. I especially wanted to see him before Miss Complicated arrived. But before I could get downstairs to breakfast, I got a call from a strange number.

"Hello?" I asked more so than stated.

"*Olá*. Is this *Senhorita* Rowan Bell?" a heavily accented voice came through the line.

"Yes," I said hesitantly. I was almost afraid to acknowledge my own name.

"This is *policial* Rodrigo Braga. I am with the *Civil do Estado do Rio de Janeiro*. You spoke with *Senhor* Batista yesterday, no?

"*Si* . . . uh . . . Yes. I did," I said, didn't want him thinking I understood Portuguese. "Is something wrong?"

My heart did a flip. Was he going to tell me I could go home? That Detective Batista didn't need me anymore? I didn't want to go home. Not yet.

"*Não,* there is nothing wrong. I was asked to call you because the manager at the Casa Nova Hotel needs to speak to you."

"They need to talk to me?" I asked. "I don't understand."

"Tell me. What is it you don't understand?" He seemed irritated.

"Why didn't they call me?"

"Do they have your phone number?"

Yeah, come to think of it, they didn't.

"Okay," I said, drawing the word out. "How did you get my phone number?"

"You must remember. You gave it to us. Wrote it down, no?"

"Oh," I said. I did remember filling out that information form while I was at the police station.

I knew they'd use it against me.

What in the world could the Casa Nova Hotel want with me?

"I don't know what they could want with me." I voiced my thoughts.

"*Si,* perhaps you forgot to pay your bill? Maybe they want *dinheiro*?"

Oh my, I thought. Do they think I was supposed to pay for that hotel room? Is that what Gerson told them? I shook my head. That didn't seem right. Why would he pay for an airline ticket for me, but not the hotel room?

Maybe he was expecting you to reimburse him . . .

OMG! This was putting a damper on my pleasant morning mood.

I took the phone away from my ear and looked at it. I was jumping to conclusions and getting upset about something I didn't even know for sure. That's what I had done yesterday thinking "G" stood for Gator.

"*Olá. Olá.*"

"*Olá.* Yes, I'm here." I had gotten lost in my thoughts. "Okay," I said. "I will go over there and see to it."

"*Si. Obrigado.* We want no trouble when it is time for you to go back to your country, no?"

I sucked my teeth.

I wasn't the one causing the trouble.

I hung up the phone and realized I could finally go down for breakfast. I was hoping that wasn't a meal that Enes skipped. I'd get him to walk me down to the hotel after we ate. Good way to digest my food and enjoy his company.

I got downstairs and found Rose in the kitchen.

"Morning," she said, a small smile forming around her lips.

"Good morning," I said, speaking loudly. I didn't know what kind of acoustics she had in the kitchen. But what I should have said to her was, "Good morning, Ms. Murder Suspect." I eyed her. Yep, I was going to have to find out more information on her today. Like her whereabouts at the time of the murder.

First, though, I needed to find out for myself what time that was . . .

"You hungry?" she asked.

"Starving."

She turned toward me. "Did you say starving?"

So, she didn't hear well in the kitchen either.

"Yes. Starving," I spit the words out.

"Good. I've got plenty of food. I'll make you a plate and bring it out to you." She turned from the skillet she hovered over. "How do you like your eggs?"

"Scrambled is fine," I said. "With cheese."

"I only have catupiry cheese." She looked at me.

"Catupiry?" I said. I scrunched my nose.

"You didn't expect I'd have American, did you?"

"No," I chuckled. "Scrambled, no cheese is fine."

"That's fine? You want the catupiry?"

"No," I said, raising my voice a decibel. "No cheese."

"Gotcha," she said. "Go sit in a booth. It'll be a couple minutes."

"Thank you," I said. I waltzed out to the front of the bar, ready to take my seat and there she was. Ms. Complicated. *Ugh!*

I knew it was her because on the other side of the booth, leaning across the table, was Enes.

She and Enes sitting in a booth near the back of the bar. Where there was less light. No intrusion from other people . . . Alone . . . Together . . . A sweet expression on Enes' face.

A sweet expression . . .

Okay, that's what I'm calling it. He looked pleased to see her. Calm. And she seemed familiar to him. Too familiar for me. I had to fight to keep from throwing up.

That wouldn't have been a pretty sight seeing there wasn't anything much but bile to come up.

I ducked back into the kitchen. All of a sudden, I'd lost my appetite.

"I told you I'd bring it out to you," Rose said when I popped back in.

"Morning." Mickey put up a hand and waved.

"Hi Mickey," I said. "Uh . . ." I turned to Rose. "I have to go over to the Casa Nova Hotel," I said. "They called me."

"You said they called you?" she asked.

"Yes." I went and stood beside her so she could read my lips. "They called me."

"Called you about what?" she asked.

That made me pause. Why did she care what it was about or that I was going over there? Unless of course she was worried about me finding some evidence of the murder she'd committed.

Allegedly committed . . .

Right, but I didn't need Enes' words in my ear at the moment

"I don't know," I told her. "They called and told me to come over." I left out the part that it was the police who had called. I didn't need her knowing I'd spoken to them, it might spook her and I wouldn't be able to get any more information out of her.

"It's not safe out there, and if something happens the police are useless." She turned her back to me and grabbed a skillet off the stove.

"I know, Enid told me that."

She turned and looked at me like her ears was still taking in what I'd said. She nodded. "Yeah, well it's true."

"Enid?" Mickey said to me.

I didn't get a chance to answer him before Rose barked out an order. "Mickey, you go over there with her. She shouldn't be walking alone. I'll try to keep your plate warm, but there are no guarantees."

I looked at Mickey. Thin. Gangly. He couldn't even handle his mother. How was he supposed to help me if someone came after me?

He smiled. "Sure, I don't mind."

No one around here ever asked me what I wanted to do. Enes assumed I needed him to get me a place to stay and now Rose thinks I need protection to go right down the street. I may not have known the name of the street I was on, but I remembered that it was the same one as the one the hotel was on.

No need of protesting.

"That'll be fine," I said and returned his smile. "I just need to run upstairs and get my purse."

"Did you see Enes?" Rose called up after me. "You should probably tell him where you're going."

This time I pretended as if I didn't hear her.

Chapter Thirteen

I really didn't need Mickey going with me. I felt safe enough. I had actually walked—okay ran—this route before. But it occurred to me I could use this as an opportunity to seek out more information about Gerson and find clues to his murder.

But first I needed to find out about Ms. Complicated.

"The weather is so nice here in Rio," I said to Mickey as we walked. I planted a big smile on my face. I wanted to try to make him comfortable with me then ease into my inquiries. I didn't know how close he and Enes were, but he might be protective about sharing personal information. Especially if he realized I was snooping for my own jealous reasons.

Did I just say "jealous?"

The morning was beautiful. Sunny, bright. It made me eager to see more of the city. I especially wanted to see the huge Christ the Redeemer statute sitting atop the peak of a mountain nestled in one of Brazil's national forests. Even without learning anything else about the city of Rio de Janeiro, I knew about that. That and Mardi Gras.

I had managed to get out of the bar without seeing Enes. I didn't know where he had disappeared to. I was happy about that. I didn't want to feel uncomfortable being around him with "her."

Her--Ms. Complicated—had still been sitting at the booth that they had shared, patiently waiting for him.

"Wait until you see how much rain we get," Mickey said in response to my nice weather comment. "You know it rains more here in the summer, but winter time, to me, is just as bad. The rain is depressing."

"But isn't it sort of like the rainforest?" I asked. "You know, it rains and then the suns comes out beaming and soaks up all the water. You don't even know it has rained."

"We get rain for days. On end."

So that was a depressing topic for him, probably not a good way to endear him to me so he'd open up. I figured I might as well come out with it.

"Who was the woman with Enes this morning, do you know?"

"He didn't introduce you?"

Oh goodness . . .

"I'm sure he would have," I said, not one bit sure about that, "but I was rushing. I wanted to get over to the hotel."

"Why do they want to see you over at the hotel, anyway?" Mickey asked.

Guess trying to get info about Ms. Complicated from Mickey was going to be a bust.

I just needed to get her and her sultry conversation with "Eric" out of my mind.

Okay, so maybe the conversation wasn't "sultry."

If she was going to be around I'd just have to accept it.

Maybe now that Ms. Complicated is here, Enes won't need your help solving the murder. No more "we" for you . . .

That would be fine with me.

I'm sure I could talk myself into really feeling that it was fine.

And I didn't have to help solve the murder to help Enes. Maybe, I'd just do it because it was what I wanted to do. Or, because it was the right thing to do. If I noticed things or found out information, it was my civic duty to report it. Even if I wasn't a civilian of the country where the murder happened.

Then I thought that to do it, I needed his help. I didn't have any information on anything that had happened. Anything that led up to Gerson's death. Anything about Gerson. And I still hadn't been able to learn what happened in Florida. I needed Enes.

In more ways than one . . .

"Hellooo." Mickey waved his hand in front of my face. "Earth to Rowan."

"Oh, sorry," I said, snapping out of my thoughts. "What did you say?"

"I asked why they want to see you over at the hotel."

"I don't know. A police officer called and told me to go over there."

"He didn't tell you why?"

"The police officer?" I asked, then answered without waiting for him to confirm. "He didn't know either."

"That's strange."

"Yeah, I thought so, too," I said.

"Are you sure?"

I let out a chuckle. "Of course I'm sure."

"Did you pay your bill?" Mickey asked.

"I didn't think I had a bill."

Mickey raised his eyebrows. "You can't stay at a hotel and not pay the bill for your room."

"I know that," I said. I didn't know how much he knew about Gerson's death or even if he knew he died in the room I was supposed to occupy. I knew that I wasn't supposed to tell how he died, but I didn't know what else I shouldn't say. Not that I knew much.

"How well did you know Gerson?" I asked, steering the conversation away from me and on to something I was more interested in. Murder.

"Gerson Crawford?"

"Yes. Gerson Crawford."

He shrugged. "I've known him all my life. So, I knew him pretty well."

"Did you live in Florida?"

"No. We're not from Florida. My mother was born in Texas."

"Were you born there, too?"

"Yeah, but I consider Rio my home."

"Did your mother get along with Gerson?"

He looked at me with narrowed eyes. "I don't know what Enes told you, but my mother wasn't mad at Gerson for what happened."

"Oh no, Enes didn't say anything to me like that. I just thought that . . ." I let my voice trail off. I didn't know what he was thinking that I knew. And maybe if I pretended like I knew what he was talking about, he might keep talking.

"I always thought Gerson was a good doctor," he added without any prompting from me. Not that I would have said anything about that.

This time it was me who shrugged. "I wouldn't know."

"How would you not know? You're friends with him, right. Well, you *were* friends with him. Wouldn't you know if he would have done that to a patient?"

A patient?

"I wouldn't think he would," I said, going along with the conversation. "I was just wondering what you thought about it."

I didn't have the faintest idea what he meant.

"I don't like talking about it," he said with a scowl on his face. "Especially since she should have been more than just a patient to him. I don't like even thinking about it. And, like I said and so you'll know, my mother doesn't blame him either or hold any grudges."

"Of course not," I said. "I wouldn't think she would."

"You don't know her," he said defensively as if I had accused her of something

"No. I don't, but . . ." I let my words trail off. This conversation definitely wasn't going how I thought it would.

"We're here," Mickey said, his demeanor changing back to the pleasant guy I'd seen in every other encounter with him. Or was he smiling because he was happy our conversation was over.

I looked up and saw the Casa Nova Hotel. I hadn't ever paid attention to how it looked. I flew in into it excited to see Kenneth, and flew out of it scared of a dead body.

Chapter Fourteen

I looked up at the tall building. The outside of the second floor covered in white stone, the upper floors in brown brick. The first floor was all glass. Covered in windows I could see a few guests in the ultra-modern lobby area. Three flags across the front. Brazil's green and black. Canada's maple leaf, and America's red, white and blue made tourists know they were welcomed.

"Hi," I said when it was my turn to walk up to the lobby desk. It was all shiny marble and hardwood. The outside brownstone, and the neighborhood of old building in need of repair belied how fancy the inside was, another thing I failed to notice when I first arrived.

"I'm Rowan Bell," I told the clerk. "I got a call from the police station today saying that you wanted to see me."

"Just a moment," she said. "I will get for you my manager."

"The police called you?" Mickey leaned in whispering, his eyes big, he waited until the clerk had walked away. "You didn't mention that."

"Just as a formality," I said. "No big deal."

"They don't do formalities down here." He took a step back from me. "Are you secretly working for them or something?"

"No," I said and frowned. "Working for them in what capacity?"

He shrugged his shoulders and seemed to coil back from me even farther.

"The hotel knew that the police could get in touch with me. That's all," I said.

I did actually have information that only the police and Enes knew. And they did say they needed me. Well, needed to talk to me, again. Maybe. Still, it appeared however inconsequential my relationship was with *a policia*, Mickey didn't like it.

"How did they know the police could reach you?" Mickey asked.

I turned and looked at him. "I don't know," I said. "Maybe because a dead person was found in my room?"

"Shhh!" The clerk had returned. She stood behind the big marble counter a sourpuss look on her face. She glanced around the lobby. "*Silêncio, pro favor.* We are not to discuss that."

Mickey snickered. "I guess not, that's even worse than the robberies."

I looked at the clerk and back at Mickey. I lowered my voice in order not to upset her even more. "What robberies?"

"There's been a rash of them. More than a few."

"At this hotel?" I asked.

"Not just here," he nodded his head toward the door. "But around here. Like they're targeting expats and things in their community."

"Bom dia" A man had appeared and stood next to the clerk. He was a man in his late forties or early fifties. His hair was still all black, but he had a strand or two of gray in his bushy moustache. "I'm Felipe, one of the managers at the Casa Nova Hotel."

"Good morning," Mickey said. Felipe frowned at him, seemingly to let him know that he wasn't speaking to him.

"Good morning," I said. Felipe's Portuguese salutation was close enough to Spanish that I understood what he was saying.

"You are Rowan Bell?"

"Yes," I said. "Is there something wrong with my bill?" It was what the police officer that called me and Mickey thought. "Because I didn't reserve the room. And you must know I didn't even stay in the room. I mean, I didn't even leave you my credit card information."

I knew I was rambling. But I didn't want to pay for a room that I hadn't requested and didn't use. I wasn't sure how much information Angie had shared with Gerson when they'd met.

I had given Angie a lot of my personal information when she set up the trip to Rio for Kenneth and I. And I just spilled all the beans when I came back with a broken heart to return the tickets. My goodness, she knew my address, where I worked, my phone number, heck even my parents phone number because I had used them as an emergency contact. And certainly she had my credit card information.

I'm sure it was against the Travel Agent's Rules of Ethical Code, if there was such a thing, to give out that kind of thing. But it seemed obvious to me that Angie didn't mind braking the rules and disseminating anything she wanted to about her clients while she played the game of pretending she was someone she wasn't.

I frowned to myself just thinking about it. And *I* was afraid to put my private information into the computer. Ha! Four-eyed Angie wasn't a cyber thief, she was an all-round thief plain and simple.

"Oh, no *Senhorita*. There is nothing wrong with your bill," Felipe was saying. "That was all taken care for you before you even arrived." He gave me the polite smile people in the service industry have. "I just needed to speak to you about a matter."

"Speak to me?"

"Yes, it won't take but a moment."

"No. That' fine," I said, my mind quickly switching gears. I couldn't think what he'd want with me, but . . ." I smiled at the thought, perhaps I could use the chance to ask the manager some questions about the murder.

"If you don't mind," he said. "I would like to speak to you in my office."

"Sure," I said.

Ah, that was even better.

"Good," he said. He looked relieved as he expected me not to oblige. "Please, just come around the counter, down that hallway, there," he pointed in the general direction, "to the door marked Office. I will let you in."

I turned to Mickey. "I'll be right back," I said. I didn't want him in on my conversation. Wasn't so sure it wasn't his mother who did the deed and he might leak information back to her if I was able to find out anything.

"You don't want me to come?" he asked. "I can translate.

"I would like to speak to you alone," Felipe the manager said. "And I speak English fine."

The use of "fine" in that sentence gave away that he really couldn't. But it certainly was good enough English that I could find out what he wanted with me and get any information I could from him.

I followed the manager's instruction, not looking back once at Mickey. I'd left him slack jaw and wide eyed.

He sure was nosey.

Felipe opened the door with the same polite smile on his face. He did a sweeping gesture. "*Por favor*, come in. Have a seat."

I took my seat and it must have electrified me, because all of a sudden I was abuzz with questions for him. "I have a question for you." I said.

"For me?"

"Yes," I said. I scooted to the end of my seat. "This is something that I've been wondering. Do you know why Gerson was in my room?"

I hadn't actually wondered that until just at that moment. All that talk about me paying the bill for the space I never occupied must have stirred it up. But it was true. Gerson was found in my room.

"What do you mean?" he asked.

"Didn't he have his own room?"

"Yes. But of course, but why he was in your room is not for me to answer." He raised an eyebrow.

It took a second, but I realized what he was saying.

"I didn't have a relationship . . ." He looked at me. "*That* kind of relationship with him. We were strictly business associates."

"Of course," he said. I could tell he wasn't convinced that we were.

"Where was his room?" I asked.

"I don't know if that is any of your concern," he said. "This is police information."

"The man was in my room. At your hotel," I said, placing my hand on my chest. I had taken on the persona of a 19th century Southern belle. Sensitive. Offended. "I can't imagine the stories I'd tell about what happened here when people ask me about my trip to Rio de Janeiro." I let out a sigh. "People lurking around in every hallway.

"Not in every hallway, *senhorita*," he said, his smile disappearing. "Mr. Crawford's room was on the tenth floor. Yours was on the third. He had come down in anticipation of your arrival." He raised those eyebrows again.

"How long had he been here?"

"He arrived the same time that he booked your room, so that would be a question that you have the answer to," he said.

I didn't know exactly when that was. It had to be around the time I left for Rome, though. But that had been a week ago. I had just received his note the day before.

"He was here alone?" I asked.

"Mr. Crawford was a private person. So I couldn't say. He didn't talk much. He did help one woman who wasn't feeling well after she ate in the restaurant. We were very grateful for that. But with the stigma of him killing his patient in Florida, we didn't want him to practice here at the hotel."

Killing his patient!

Is that what Mickey meant about his mother not holding a grudge? She knew the person he killed? And that person was his patient?

"And back to you disparaging remark about our hotel," he was still talking, "the police feels as if someone may have followed him down to your room. It was probably someone he knew. Probably someone from America."

"Someone followed him down there?"

"I think if you are interested in more information on this you should ask Mr. Crawford."

My eyes got big. Was he telling me to speak to the dead?"

"Mr. Enes Crawford, his brother. He was to meet his brother in that room as well, from what I understood. In anticipation of your arrival."

"Oh," I said.

So, Enes was supposed to be in that room, too, when I met Gerson.

"If that is all the questions you have, there is the matter I requested your presence," he said. His smile a little weaker than it had been. "There have unfortunately been several robberies . . . uh . . . Here. Related or unrelated, we're not sure, to the uptick of crimes in the area."

"Yes, I heard about that."

"Not to worry," he sat up a little straighter in his seat. "We value our guests' safety and the safety of their things. We have taken every precaution."

I nodded and smiled.

"Mr. Crawford, aware of that, took a precaution himself," Felipe the manager continued.

"His own precaution?" I asked. Evidently he hadn't been too careful, he ended up dead.

"Concerning you," he said, as if he read my thoughts. "Well, your belongings."

"He did?" I said, not knowing what he was talking about.

"We have a package for you."

"A package?" I felt my knees buckle, good thing I was sitting down. I just couldn't do with anymore surprise letters from anyone.

"Yes," he said and pulled open one of the desk drawers. "This, I believe belongs to you." He had one of those brown envelopes in his hand. The same kind that the ticket and room key had arrived in, but this one was much thicker. "We would have passed it on to the police," he said, "but he left it for you long before the . . . uh . . . *Incidente*."

I wanted to say "murder not incident," but I was too intrigued about what Gerson had left for me and getting back to share it with Enes.

At the time he died, he thought I was a private eye. Maybe it had information about the murder in Florida in it.

"What's in it?"

"That is for you to see," he said. "For me, I just deliver it.

I reached my hand out for it, but he pulled it back.

"I will need you to sign for it." He reached into another drawer and took out a piece of paper. "And of course I will need to see some identification before I can release to you."

"Of course," I said.

I'd be willing to do just about anything to get my hands on it so I could see what things Gerson wanted to tell me.

Chapter Fifteen

I finally got the envelope out of his grubby little hands. I held onto it tightly as I threw my ID down into the bottom of my purse.

I scrambled to get out of his office as fast as I could, I didn't want him having second thoughts on letting me have it.

I rounded the corner coming out of the office and ran right smack into a woman. I dropped the envelope and had bent down to pick it up before I realized whom I'd run into.

"Enid?" I said stooping to pick it up. "Hi."

She took a step back and looked at me. "Hi," she said. "What are you doing here?" She turned and looked around behind her.

"The police called and told me the hotel wanted to talk to me. They wanted to make sure I was okay."

"The police?" she asked a surprised look on her face. "Didn't I tell you to stay clear of them?"

"Oh, I didn't tell you, I guess. Well, I know for sure I didn't tell you," I said. I turned and looked behind me as well. I didn't want the manager to hear me speaking to a guest of the hotel, if Enid was one, about something he had asked me not to speak about. But Enid had helped me. The only one to talk to me when I went into the bar the day before.

"I was registered to stay in this hotel. But when I arrived yesterday, I found a dead body."

"You?" her eyes got big and she pointed at me with her finger. "You found it? Wow."

"Yeah, I know," I said nodding my head. "In my hotel room. Very frightening."

"So is that what you were upset about yesterday? When I saw you?" she asked.

"Yes. It was." I nodded.

"Oh my," she said, putting her hand up to her cheek. "I can't imagine that happening to me. What did you see?"

I felt comfortable talking to Enid. In fact, out of the people I'd met so far in Rio, including the hotel manager, I trusted her. But I had been told not to share information about the murder with anyone. Not that I knew very much. But I did know from my television shows that holding onto, and keeping quiet about key information was pertinent to solving the crime.

"I was too scared to look at anything," I lied. "And I'm really still upset about it." I swallowed hard and tucked my head. "I don't even like talking about it." I was trying hard to stick to my promise.

She gave me a look that said she wasn't sure if she believed me. "So the hotel called you in to ask you about that?"

"No, they had something for me," I said and looked down at the envelope I still had in my hand.

"They gave you that?" she pointed to the brown package.

"Yeah," I said, then stuffed it inside my purse. I wanted to wait until I got to Enes before I opened it. I wanted to share all my "clues" with him. "What are you doing here?" I asked turning the conversation away from the envelope.

"My boyfriend works here," she said. "I'm just waiting for him to get off."

"I see," I said. "I turned and looked down the back hallway, figuring that must be an employee's entrance. "Are you coming over to the bar today?"

"So what's in the envelope?" she asked, turning the conversation right back around.

I hunched my shoulders. "I don't know," I said. "I haven't opened it yet. I think the person who reserved the room for me left it."

"The person?" She chuckled. "Don't you know who reserved your room for you?"

"I do now," I said. I was beginning to feel like such a gossiper. I knew I needed to just keep my mouth closed. I didn't want to do anything to upset Enes, even though he was upsetting me hanging out with Ms. Complicated. "But I really can't talk about it. You understand."

"Oh, sure I do," she waved her hand to say forget she asked me any questions. "This is all so surreal," she said. "Dead bodies, mysterious envelopes. Is your life always this exciting?"

I chuckled. "No, it's not. And I must admit," I leaned in close to her, "I never imagined any of this to happen. I came to Rio, by myself, to meet someone that didn't show and got tangled up in a murder mystery."

"A murder mystery, huh?" She turned her head and looked at me out the side of her eye. "You're not thinking about trying to solve it, are you?"

I laughed. "I have found out a few things that made me curious." I patted my purse. "And who knows what else I might learn."

"You just be careful," she said. "Rio is no place to venture out and especially not to try and solve a murder."

"Oh no," I said. "I'll be careful. You know," I changed the subject again, "I wanted to apologize to you about yesterday."

"Apologize?" she said. "For what?"

"You know, about the name thing," I said. "Giving you a fake name. I was just nervous. I had just been in a bad situation."

"Forget about it," she dismissed it with a wave of her hand. "I completely understand." She smiled.

"How about we start again?" I said. I stuck out my hand. "I'm Rowan Bell."

"Nice to meet you, Rowan Bell," she said.

We laughed.

"You know," she said. "I had thought about stopping by the bar today to check on you. So I'm glad I ran into you."

"Me too," I said. It was nice to have a friend who was a woman and around my age.

"So listen. How about if I help you get your head out of all this sleuthing business that you're sticking your nose in? My boyfriend and I work part-time for a tour company and I'm on the schedule this afternoon."

"You do tours?" I asked.

"Yep. We take groups out to the Tijuca Forest National Park to see the art deco statute of Jesus. You know, the one Rio is famous for. We go to Sugar Mountain the landscape there is unbelievable. We also do walking tours through a favela."

"A favela," I said. After Rose's story about Emilie and Joseph, I definitely wanted to see that. Everything she mentioned was something I wanted to see.

"I was wondering-"

I didn't even let her finish. "I would love to go," I said, practically jumping with giggles. "Wait," I dialed back my enthusiasm. "You were inviting me to go, right?"

"Yes," she said and chuckled. "But listen," she started speaking hurriedly, "I have to get ready for the group. I'm going to send my boyfriend to meet you. Is that okay?"

"Sure," I said.

"Hey Rowan," I heard a voice call out. "I've been waiting for you. You were taking so long." It was Mickey. He'd come down the hallway to find me.

"Hey. I have to go," Enid said, walking as she was speaking. "My boyfriend's name is Afonso. He'll be there in about an hour."

"Okay, thanks Enid." I waved at her. "See you in a bit."

"Oh, that's Enid?" Mickey said, still making his way over to me. He turned and watched as she went past him and made her way down the hall.

"I thought you were going to wait for me in the lobby."

"Didn't you hear me?" he said and looked at me. "I just said you were taking too long."

"Well, I'm ready to go now." I started walking toward the lobby.

"What was it that Manager Felipe wanted with you?"

"Nothing. Just wanted to express his condolences."

"For Gerson?"

"Yep," I said and pushed open the glass doors.

"So wait," he said following out the door behind me. "Were you dating both of them?"

Chapter Sixteen

"We're back," I announced. I had swung open the door to the bar and marched in. Mickey and I hadn't spoken all the way back.

I didn't know what kind of girl he thought I was, and he didn't seem to have any useful information for me. I wasn't angry with him. Just moving on.

"I was getting worried about you."

I smelled him. I took in a whiff and turned around. Enes. He had come up from behind me, evidently he was now occupying one of the booths at the front of the bar.

"I had Mickey with me," I said and smiled, looking up at him. "He protected me."

Mickey looked back at me. He was making his way to the bar. "Yep. Sure did," he said, his words coming out dry.

The woman, Ms. Complicated, was nowhere in sight. I hoped she left, but I did keep my eye on the restroom area to make sure she didn't come popping up out of there.

"Well just don't go off on any more excursions. I'm supposed to be keeping you safe." He pulled his phone out of his pocket and looked at it. "I'm going to talk to Jorge in a bit. See if we can't get you home."

I nodded. "When are you going home?" Usually I wasn't that bold when talking to men.

"Probably around the same time as you," he said. "My mother wants me to hurry back."

"Oh," I said. "I thought you were going to look into what happened to your brother?"

He smiled down at me.

"You two, sit." Rose came over, her usual force-of-nature-self and pushed me toward the booth where it looked like he'd just occupied. There was a cup of coffee. The cup was still full, but it looked cold.

Enes followed behind us, an amused look on his face.

"Miss Rowan ran out of here this morning without breakfast, and Enes I haven't seen you eat since you got here." She shook her head. "No one's getting sick on my watch. You both have to keep up your strength." She set plates in front of both of us. "I don't usually do this."

I looked down. It looked like turkey sandwiches with cheese. American cheese.

I smiled up at her. "Thank you," I said.

"I'm not hungry," Enes said.

"Eat," Rose directed, pointing at the sandwich. She swiped the cup of coffee off the table. "What'dya two want to drink?"

"I'll take a ginger ale," I said. "If you have it."

"Of course I do. What's a bar without ginger ale?"

Enes chuckled. "I guess I'll have one, too. To go with my . . . What is this . . ." he looked at the time on his phone again. "My brunch."

"Call it whatever you want," Rose said. "Just eat it."

Enes laid the phone down on the table. Then with his eyes planted squarely on Rose, he took a huge bite of his sandwich.

"Good," she said. "I'll be right back with your drinks."

"I heard you went back to the hotel," Enes said.

"They called me." I picked up my sandwich. "Well, not the hotel. The police." I swung my head back and forth. "The hotel called the police so they could call me."

"I get it," he said. "You filled out that information form."

"Right. So they had my number." I took a bite of my sandwich, then covered my mouth, chewing and talking at the same time. "They had something that Gerson had left for me."

Enes' eyes got big. "Really? What is it?"

I was already digging down in my purse to give it to him. "This."

He stared at it for a second. "What's inside?"

"I don't know." I poked it at him, signaling for him to take it. "Must have something to do with the murder in Florida because the manager at the hotel said Gerson had given it to him a while before . . . You know."

He took the envelope from me, but instead of opening it, he laid it on the table.

"So now you've had your morning excursion. You'll stay put while I go to the police station?"

"No. I'm going out again. Sightseeing."

"With who?" It was Rose who asked. She was back at the table.

"With Enid."

"Who is Enid?" Enes and Rose said it both practically at the same time. It was like being around my parents.

"You know Enid," I said. "She was sitting with me yesterday when I first came in. You told her to see about me."

"I did no such thing," Rose said. "I don't know who she is."

"Yes, you do," I said. "I just said to you this morning that she told me that the police couldn't be trusted and you said she was right."

"I did?" she said.

"Well, you said 'that' would be right."

"Oh," she nodded. "I remember that. "But I thought you said *Enes* had told you that. You know I don't hear too well in the kitchen."

"So you don't-" I stopped in the middle of my sentence. Ms. Complicated was sauntering out from the back of the bar.

I thought she was gone. Shoot!

"Ah, Rose, I see you got Eric to eat," Ms. Complicated said.

Oh, wasn't she just so familiar with him.

And why does she call him Eric?

"Wasn't me. It was Rowan," Rose said. She winked at me.

I had to keep from giggling. She was taking up for me. Maybe Rose wasn't the murderer after all.

"Rowan? Have I met her, Eric?"

That turkey and cheese was going to come out of my stomach and right back on that plate if I had to listen to her for another minute.

I looked her. She was a "looker" as my mother would say. She had long, dark auburn hair. No make-up her white skin was flawless, no marks or freckles. She was slim and carried herself as if she fit just right in her skin.

"Rowan, this is Ava Sheely. She's a detective from Tallahassee. I know her from the neighborhood."

I couldn't speak, there were too many things going on in my head just from those few words he'd said.

First, he'd said she was from Tallahassee, "the neighborhood." Did that mean he lived in Tallahassee? Was *my* neighbourhood *his* neighborhood?

OMG! That had to be kismet.

And then, well this one should've been the number one thing—when he introduced us, he said my name first. She was the one who said she didn't know me, but he introduced *me* to *her*. That must mean something.

And second . . . Wait, I was turning into Rose . . . third, he said she was a detective. Did that mean she was only in Rio in her capacity as someone who could help solve the murder? Is that what "I can do complicated meant?"

"She doesn't talk much, huh?" Ava said.

I snapped out of my reverie, a crazy little grin on my face, they probably thought I was a little demented.

"It's nice to meet you, Ava," I said. "I'm from Tallahassee, too," I said.

"Oh, is this who you were talking about, Eric?" she asked Enes acting coy.

He was talking about me? God I hoped it was something good.

"Why does she call you Eric?" I said, looking over at him.

"That's my name when I'm home," he said.

"Portuguese isn't good enough for him when he's in Florida," Rose said.

"That's not true," Enes said. He shrugged. "Just thought it'd make me more Americanized."

"Hi. I'm looking for Rebecca," a man came in the door said. He definitely was Brazilian. He was dark, exotic looking and stood at least six feet tall.

"Don't know that person," Rose said. "Look around and see if you see her."

"I don't know her either," he said. "My girlfriend, Enid sent me for her."

"Oh," I said. "Are you Afonso?"

"Yes," he smiled at me. "You Rebecca, no?"

I just nodded. No need to explain my lies again.

He nodded back. "Ready to see the beautiful sights of my country?"

"Yes," I said. "I'm ready."

"Okay. Okay," he said, a big grin on his face. "But first I need *o banheiro*."

"Back there," both Rose and Enes answered and pointed.

He, backing up, bowed his head, nodding then turned and headed to the back.

"You can't go with him," Enes said.

"I'm not," I said. "Not really. I'm going with Enid. That's just her boyfriend."

"Who is Enid?" Rose asked.

We'd already been through this I thought. "You know Enid," I said.

"I know Enid," Mickey called from his barstool, and held up a hand. I never saw him with a drink. He just sat there. "Just saw her at the Casa Nova Hotel."

"See," I said.

"I don't know . . ." Enes said.

Leaning across the table, I put the tips of my finger on his phone and slid it closer to him. I'd noticed he had an iPhone just like me the first time he pulled it out. "You can put a tracker on your phone for me." I told him just like I told my parents. "And if you want to know where I am, you'll be able to see me beeping right at you."

Chapter Seventeen

Had I just flirted with Enes?

I think I had. I flirted with him and I did it right in front of Ava! He'd put his password in and slid his phone, mimicking what I'd had done, over toward me. I didn't waste any time putting my phone information into the app. He smiled at me the whole time.

I was smiling, too.

I felt proud of myself.

So proud that we'd been riding for a while before I looked up. I was in the front seat of Afonso's Fiat. It was old and rusty, nothing like Enes', but I had happily slid right into it.

"What's that?" I asked. I pointed to a mountain filled with colorful houses. Okay, maybe it wasn't a mountain, but each row of houses sat higher than the last.

"A favela," he said.

"Oh," I said smiling. "Is that what it looks like? It's different. Nothing like the projects at home."

He grunted.

"Where are we meeting Enid?" I asked. We were getting close to the tour destination. I would have thought that we'd meet at the tours office. "Where are all the tourists?"

He looked at me, this time he growled.

Oh, he's not too pleasant, I thought. I wondered what kind of tour guide he was.

Probably not a good one . . .

I looked at him, and now he looked different than he had before. He looked greasy. Slick hair, shiny leathery skin. It looked as if he'd baked in the sun twenty-four hours a day. I looked at his hands on the steering wheel. His nails were dirty. I leaned in and secretly took a whiff of him. Ewww! He smelled like week old tobacco and perspiration mixed.

Had he been at work and the sleek and modern Casa Nova Hotel looking and smelling like that?

Right then, I began to feel a cause for concern.

"Where did you say we were meeting Enid?" I asked again.

"You will see her soon," he said. "And you'd be better off not asking me so many questions."

Grouch . . .

I turned my attention out of the window and watched as we got closer and closer to the favela. The slum of it became apparent as we neared. The bright colors that had impressed me from afar, close up were faded. The tenement houses were crumbling and there were people and dogs hanging in the street. Eyes watching us as we drove by, seemingly in anticipation of us stopping to speak with them. One of my kindergarteners had told me those that waited on corners and scoped out passers-by, were dope boys.

The wisdom of a five-year-old . . .

Afonso made me nervous, but the neighbourhood, it was making me anxious. Surely a "walking" tour wouldn't venture this far up into the area.

"I thought we were going on a tour? Where is everyone else?" I turned and looked at Afonso. "Where is Enid?"

"You're going to see her now," he said and pulled over. He got out the car, slamming the door behind him.

I looked out of the window. I didn't want to get out. I didn't see any tour group. I didn't see anything worth seeing. I didn't see Enid.

Then I heard her voice.

"Get her out of the car." Her voice angry. Mean. Different from any other time I'd heard her speak.

My door came opened, scaring me. "Out!" Afonso said.

"What's going on?" I said not moving. I felt like I was about to pee on myself.

"If you don't get out of that car," Enid said. "You'll wish you had."

I had gotten so scared now that I didn't think I could move. My knees were shaking, my hands were trembling, and I could feel the sweat running down my face.

"What do you want with me?" I said, my voice cracking, my words were hardly audible.

"You got something we need," Afonso said.

"Not out here," Enid said. "Get her inside."

Afonso grabbed my arm and yanked me out of the car. It hurt and upset me, but I supposed that if he hadn't, I wouldn't have been able to get out on my own volition.

I walked between them as entered one of the buildings. We made our way up a narrow hallway with concrete steps and walls. It was dark and musty. Up two flights, Afonso pulled me down a hallway and flung me into an apartment that Enid had unlocked.

"What is going on?" I asked, tears streaming down my face. I was practically pleading with Enid.

"Where's that envelope you had today?" she asked me.

I patted my purse, thinking I could give it to her and this nightmare would be over. Then I remembered I had given it to Enes.

I swallowed hard. "I don't have it," I said.

"Where is it?" Afonso said.

"You don't want to mess with him," Enid snarled. "You've never suffered that much pain."

"I'm telling the truth," I said. "I-I left it at the bar."

"What was in it?" she asked.

"I don't know."

"You're lying," she said.

"I'm not." My voice went up a couple of octaves, and I nearly shouted out the words. "I didn't open it. I didn't have time before he," I jerked my head toward Afonso, "came to pick me up."

"Why were you there to meet Gerson?"

"Gerson?" I said confused. "I wasn't there to meet Gerson. He's dead-"

"I know he's dead," Enid spat the words at me. "Before he died. Why were you meeting Gerson before he got bashed in the head?" She was so mad the words had to be forced out of her mouth. "You came to Rio to see him."

"Oh." I started shaking my head. I couldn't tell if I was trembling that hard, or trying to get her to understand that I wasn't trying to keep anything from her. "He thought I was someone else."

"Don't make me have Afonso get the answers out of you." She came and stood over me. "He'll knock you upside your head. See if that'll help you to tell me the truth." She poked me with her finger. "You'll be sorry you just didn't do it in the first place."

"I-I'm telling the truth," I said, so scared I couldn't hardly think. "He thought I could help him solve a murder back in the states."

"Ask her about her visit to the police station," Afonso said.

I looked at him, and then at Enid.

What were they trying to get out of me?

"What did you tell the police?" she said.

"About what?" I asked.

"About Gerson's murder?" she said, walking the length of the floor then turning back.

Surely she didn't think I was able to give the police any kind of pertinent information. Heck, the whole time I thought it was Kenneth.

All these questions they were hurling at me made my head spin. I was dizzy. Confused. I shook my head to clear it, the sweat flinging from my face.

I didn't understand what they was getting at. Why did they care about Gerson's murder or what was in the envelope?

Then it hit me.

I looked at her. Fright and surprise engulfing me. I couldn't believe it had been her.

"How do *you* know Gerson was hit in the head?" I asked her.

"What?" She spun around and glared at me.

"You saw me leave that hotel room, didn't you? Then you followed me to the bar," I said. I looked at Afonso and back at her. "Were you two somewhere watching what was going on?"

"What are you talking about?" she said.

"That wasn't wine on your blouse when I met you yesterday, was it?"

"Shut up!" she screamed at me.

She started pacing around the room like a caged animal. It probably wasn't a good idea for me to egg her on, but everything had started to click.

"That was blood," I shouted. "Gerson's blood." I blinked my eyes and tried to remember the day before when I'd met her. "And," my eyes followed her as she paced, "you tried to get me to go with you yesterday, didn't you? Trying to pretend you were going to take me to the Embassy. You thought then I'd seen something. You were planning on kidnapping me yesterday."

"I said for you to shut up," she said getting close to my face. "Or you'll end up like him."

"The two of you killed Gerson! You're murderers!"

She coiled back from me, stood up straight, and seemed to have a calm come over her at those words being said aloud. A wicked grin curled around her lips. "Yes we killed him! You're a smart one, aren't you?"

I shook my head in disgust at her.

"And yes," she said throwing up her hand, "I thought you knew something and I wanted to get it out of you." Her words were cold.

"Don't tell her anything," Afonso said. "You're admitting all this to her. What it wrong with you?"

"It doesn't matter. She won't be able to tell anyone any of this."

I narrowed my eyes at her. For some reason, I wasn't afraid. Maybe it the calm that comes over a person right before they die. And yes, I was expecting to die. Or maybe, I just didn't want my last minutes on Earth to be that of a Scared Nelly.

"Why did you kill him?" I asked.

"You want to know why?" she said, spurting out the words. "I'll tell you why. He caught us robbing the place. The fancy-smancy Casa Nova Hotel. They treated my man like nothing!" She flung a finger over toward Afonso.

"So we got our due," she was on a roll now, talking without me saying a word. "What was coming to us. That's all. But Mr. Perfect," her words were filled with venom against Gerson, "who was a wanted felon, decides he needs to inform the law about us. Our crimes were nothing compared to his."

"You don't know that he actually killed someone," I said. "That had only been alleged against him."

"That's crazy talk," she said. "He wouldn't have come down here if he were innocent. He deserved what happened to him."

"Why did you come after me?"

"He told us that he'd told his investigator about us. He'd just got off the phone with *her*, he'd said. We knew it was a woman, and then here you come, key in hand, and walked right in."

"But he hadn't called me. He didn't even have my phone number," I said. "He only knew my name and the name of the hotel in Rome where I was staying."

She looked over at Afonso, showing perhaps regret in her eyes, but when she looked back at me, I saw nothing but hatred. "Looks like you were in the wrong place at the wrong time."

That much, I knew was true.

"And now you're going to have to pay for it. Just your luck," Enid said. "Too bad you're that stupid. Instead of sticking around, you've should have gone back where you came from."

"I'm not the one who's stupid," I said. "You had gotten away with it. Enes didn't think they'd ever find the murderer. I don't even think they had any evidence. Everyone thought it was random. Now you've kidnapped me and are planning . . . I guess, to kill me. Now that's stupid. Everyone knows I left to go with you."

"No one in that bar knows me."

Yeah, now I wished I had listened to them when they told me that.

"And no one will ever find you in this favela," she said wickedly.

And then, with dread slowly closing in on me, I remembered the tracker I'd put on Enes' phone and knew he would see me beeping at him.

I just hoped he would make it to me in time.

Epilogue

It didn't take Enes long to come and get me. Thank God. Rose told me later that he hadn't even waited fifteen minutes after I'd left to get on my trail.

The red dot, according to Rose, stayed in one place too long. Sightseers should be on the move. And with Mickey saying Enid had ducked out as soon as he appeared down that hallway at the Casa Nova Hotel, everyone had thought her saying she was a regular at the bar when she wasn't, then sending her boyfriend for me was fishy.

I didn't even mind that he'd brought Ava along for backup. That ended up being a good thing, because she had to hold Enid and Afonso at gunpoint until the Brazilian coppers got there, once I told him that they were his brother's killers.

After Enid and Afonso were arrested and charged with Gerson's murder, Detective Jorge Batista, donning his good cop persona, told me I was free to go home to Florida. But before I left, I made sure to find out if Enes and Ava were an item. I didn't want to be back in Midspring pining for a man that was already tied up in a relationship.

The answer to that? A resounding, "No!"

I never found out what was in that envelope. Enes said we should leave that for another day, we'd both gone through enough. But I did think that he may have shared its contents with Ava. I hadn't been sure how I felt about that, until I realized exactly what he was saying. Ha!

Leaving it for another day meant we would see each other again.

Well, at least that was what I hoped it meant. Prayed it meant. Crossed my fingers that that was what it meant.

I caught a plane to Tallahassee the next morning. Two days in Rio had seemed like an eternity. And it had definitely changed my life.

I didn't call my parents and tell them I was coming because I needed to digest everything that had happened, and have time to recuperate. I knew they'd just bombard me with questions.

But, when I got to the airport, there they were waiting in the baggage claim area for me. My mother, with her cell phone in hand, waved it wildly as she ran in my direction.

The End

BED & BREAKFAST BEDLAM

Read chapters from the first in my
Logan Dickerson Cozy Mystery Series.

Then get the ebook for FREE at your
favorite online book retailer!

Prologue

Every day is the first day of the rest of your life.

Or so the saying goes. But most times, I'd say ninety-nine percent of the time, your life goes pretty much as you plan it – or don't plan it. Mundane everyday sort of stuff. You go to college, get married, have kids – or not. On a small scale the daily happenings in a person's life are pretty much inconsequential and certainly not leading to anything monumental. But when viewed through the backdrop of history, sometimes, some of those insignificant, trivial day-to-day kinds of things have colossal after-effects.

For instance, the Archduke Ferdinand deciding to visit injured patients at a local hospital, and Gravilo Princip just happening to visit a certain café at the same time. Those innocuous decisions ultimately led to Princip assassinating Ferdinand and the start of World War I.

Or, the small chunk of debris innocently traveling through space that found Planet Earth in its path a few million years ago. It, in a one-in-four-hundred-billion chance, struck in the exact spot where its impact could cause the extinction of all the dinosaurs (although my mother has a different theory about that), making us have to spend tens of years and tens of thousands of dollars to dig them up just to find out what they looked like.

Archaeologists, like me, mark time around such events. Like BCE or AD (before the Common Era, although I prefer Before Christ denoted as BC, and

Anno Domini). Or like denoting an age, or period (like Victorian and Jurassic). Usually though, such history marking events happen over long periods, and are not classified as distinct times in our history until long after they occur.

But for me, the mammoth event that completely changed the course of my history, happened over the period of just one week. And it only took me one day to realize it.

What marked the complete and utter change in the course of my ordinary life? It was the death of a total stranger.

Chapter One
Track Rock Gap
Gainesville, Georgia

Wednesday Night, BGD (Before Gemma Died)

My heart was beating out of my chest.

I stood with my back against the outside wall of a small wooden shed, sweat dripping down my face, and tried to slow down my racing heart. I knew if I didn't, the sound of it thumping would give away my position.

"How am I going to get out of this?" I muttered

I felt my legs trembling, my palms were clammy, and my whole body was reeling in a flood of fear. I bent over, resting my hands on my knees, while trying to catch my breath, and prayed. It seemed as if I could almost hear God saying in response, "That's what you get, Logan."

I should have listened to my mother.

My mother had told me not to go poking my nose (or the rest of me for that matter) into federally protected lands. But still, at nearly thirty, I had to rail against her advice just to prove I was capable of managing my life without her interference.

Look where that got me.

I peeked my head around the shed and tried to focus my eyes through the darkness.

Two U.S. Forest Service officers were shining their flashlights on the metal heap I had upended. It seemed I didn't have the criminal savvy or cat-like moves that I thought I had. Clumsy didn't even start to describe the maze of mishaps that led me to my current predicament.

I slid down the wall, crouching, I swiped the back of my hand across my forehead, and narrowed my eyes, searching for a way out.

Hopefully, there was one.

I was at the Track Rock Gap ruins in Gainesville, Georgia. I had been here before – on the other side of the locked gate – as an archaeologist looking for ancient Maya ruins with my mother.

At some point, thousands of years ago, the Maya population disappeared from Central America. Many archaeologists believed that they died *en masse*. But being more like my mother than I ever cared to admit, I had a different theory. While excavating in Belize, my mother and I discovered clues that lead us to believe that the Maya may have migrated to, and lived in, Georgia. At Track Rock Gap to be exact.

When we checked it out, word had gotten around the area that Maya ruins laid up the side of a steep mountainside inside Track Rock Gap that was comprised of more than a 150 stone masonry walls with Mayan-like inscriptions, evidence of agricultural terraces, and remains of what could have been a sophisticated irrigation system. Just like what was found in the jungles of Mesoamerica at every Maya site excavated.

But if the Maya had settled in America, the U.S. government didn't want anyone to know about it.

When my mother and I first arrived we found Track Rock Gap locked tight with big "KEEP OUT" signs plastered everywhere. So we left. My mother's scientific need to know not even stirred. Mine, however, was screaming for answers. I just had to know why anyone would keep possible proof of a Maya civilization in Georgia secret, so I decided to come and check it out – trespassing laws be damned.

Now I was being chased by two federal officers for my callous disregard of my government's edicts. And to top it off I still didn't have any more information about the Maya-American occupation I came to out. But, at this moment, I realized that I no longer had any interest in where they lived, whatsoever.

I'm sure that had to do with the fact that now my curiosity was going to get me thrown in jail. Or worse, a federal prison.

My recon skills were nowhere as good as my excavation ones. I hadn't been able to get a map of the area, and I came armed only with a flashlight and my iPhone 6. Neither one turned out to be any help. Before I was more than a hundred yards into the site, I had knocked over the shed. A metal one that creaked and clanked as it fell with a loud thud spitting dirt everywhere. It scared me and I took off running. As it turned out, I ran in the same direction the guards were emerging from. I did a one eighty and slid the last few feet behind the shed where I now stooped. Thank God they hadn't seen me.

I peered around the shed. The two guards were still examining the metal pile of heap. They were kicking it with the toe of their shoes.

Maybe they'd think some vermin knocked it over. Or, maybe they'd think it fell by itself. It hadn't been very sturdy. I barely touched it.

"Is anyone there? Show yourself," one of the guards yelled.

Crap.

I turned back around and closed my eyes. I knew I couldn't just stand still and let them catch me, I had to make a run for it.

Plus, I had to pee.

That was going to make running anywhere pretty difficult.

I opened my eyes to survey what was close and spotted a trailer about thirty yards out. With the light that emanated from the trailer, I could see that just beyond it was a tangle of bushes and trees. A place I could escape in darkness and the noises of the night, and through them, I hoped, was the road out.

But I needed to distract Uncle Sam's watchmen.

I closed my eyes and asked for strength. Even though my mother was a lot closer to God than I was, and I typically went against her, I was hoping He'd give me some slack.

Pulling in a quick breath and holding it, I threw a rock as hard as I could in the opposite direction of where I needed to go.

"Did you hear that?" one guard said to the other.

"What?"

"Thought I heard something over there." He pointed in the direction I threw the rock. "We'd better check it out." They took off one way and I took off running in the other.

I landed behind the small camper-like building. There was a dim light on inside. I peeped through a window and discovered that the place must be the guard station. There were two desks, some chairs, a microwave and a coffeemaker. The light I'd seen was from a computer screen.

Yep. This was where they hung out when vandals, like me, weren't on the prowl in their protected lands.

I wonder what kind of jail time federal trespassing carries? I let out a sigh.

Looked like my recognition wasn't going to come from brilliant work in the field of Maya archaeology but from my stupid mistakes off the grid. This was going to ruin my reputation as an archaeologist. The small one that I had.

I looked up at the darkened sky and thanked God there was little moonlight. Darkness was a good cover. I spied the start of the dense bushes that lined the perimeter only a few yards away, then took one more look in the direction the guards had gone. After I felt I was clear, I fell flat on my belly and slithered across the dirt and patches of grass to the trees. I rolled over on my back once I reached them, I raised up my hand at the pale moon and said softly, "I will, in no way, shape, or form, ever break the law again. I absolutely and solemnly swear."

Now to get out of Track Rock Gap and walk – *nay* – run the mile and a half

down the road to where I had parked my
car.

Chapter Two
Itza, Georgia

Early Thursday Morning, BGD
I settled my bill at the small motel I had stayed at first thing. After nearly getting caught trespassing the night before, I didn't want to waste any time beating it out of town. Not that I thought they knew who I was or that they could find me. Still it made me a little nervous being so close to the memory of my illegal activities.

I headed out to the parking lot, knapsack over my shoulder, pulling my luggage behind me, I walked at a brisk pace. I slowed down as I passed the glass-encased office. The door to the small room was open. Eyes straightforward, I wanted to appear calm – normal. I'd smile and wave if the clerk looked up at me. That was when I heard "him."

"Logan Dickerson," he said. "You said her name is Logan Dickerson?"

I stopped dead in my tracks.

What the hey?

"That's right. She came in last night. Covered in dirt," the woman at the counter was saying. "She looked real suspicious like."

My heart stopped. How did that woman see me come in? That little . . . toothless . . . old snoop. She had a big mouth. Telling some unknown man stuff about me. He could be a stalker. Someone out to kill me. I tried to peek through the door and get a better look at him.

Who was he anyway?

My heart started beating again – pounding actually – in my ears. It was so loud that I couldn't hear a word they were saying. So I moved in closer, stilled myself, and tilting my head I listened.

"Last night you say?" he asked.

I couldn't hear her answer, but she must have said, yes.

"What does she look like?" he asked.

Don't tell him, big mouth. Don't. Tell. Him.

"She's black, like you. Shoulder length hair. Light skinned. Not skinny. Not fat."

Crap.

"And how long has she been here?"

Was there no end to his questions?

"Two nights," the woman blabbed.

Oh my goodness, I thought. *She's gotta be breaking some kind of privacy law telling that man all my business.*

"Did she kill somebody?" Blabbermouth asked.

"No," he said and chuckled.

"Then how come the FBI is looking for her?"

FBI? Oh my God! I am going to jail.

"Where is she now?" he asked, seemingly ignoring her question.

"Don't know. Still in her room I'm guessing 'cause that's her jeep over there. The white one."

I looked over at my car.

Now I'm going to have to dump it.

"Yes. I know that's her vehicle," he said. "We have it on video. That's how we found her."

Video?

"Well, you better hurry up if'n you aim to catch her."

"Why is that ma'am?" he asked.

"She paid up her bill right before you showed up. I think she's getting ready to make a run for it."

Oh, she was so right about that.

I couldn't listen anymore. I had to get out of there. But I wasn't sure if I should head for the car – the one they had on video – or just start running.

I saw a dumpster.

I could jump into it and hide.

I looked down at myself. I had on jeans, a navy Polo jacket with a white shell underneath and tennis shoes.

Definitely dumpster-diving clothes.

I put my knapsack on the ground and took off my jacket. Using the sleeves, I tied it around my waist. Then I took the ponytail holder off my wrist and pulled my long hair back, looping it around. I needed to be aerodynamically poised to make my get away as fast as possible.

I was just going to run for it. Head to the car I decided. He didn't know what I looked like. Just that I was black. He wouldn't know it was me until I got into my car.

I stepped off the sidewalk onto the asphalt of the blacktop parking lot. I was sure I could make it to my car before he noticed me. I kept my eyes on my Jeep.

Why did I park so far?

I twisted my neck slightly to the left and from the corner of my eye, I saw FBI guy come out of the office door. He headed right, toward the room I had just vacated.

I picked up my pace.

Not much farther. I can do this.

I *can* do this.

I turned my neck to the right, looked over my shoulder, and just then his gaze caught mine.

Crap.

"Logan Dickerson," he shouted.

I started running.

Maybe he'll think I'm hard of hearing.

Trying to break into federally-guarded lands had been a bad idea, just as my mother warned. But who was she to talk? She had probably broken all kinds of laws and been involved with federal cover-ups and murders over the past few years.

I looked over my shoulder and there was FBI guy gaining on me. Yep. My mother was certainly no shining example and, to be honest, it was probably her fault that I turned out to have these criminal proclivities. Bad parenting.

"Hey! Stop!"

I ran toward my car, my luggage hitting every bump and hole, turning over off its wheels. Fumbling, I pointed the clicker and unlocked the door. I grabbed the handle and turned to see that he'd practically caught up with me.

Crap. Crap. Crap.

Before I could get my door open I felt his hand on my arm. Even though I knew he was there, it startled me and I jumped.

"Hey. Didn't you hear me calling you? he asked.

I was breathing hard. He didn't even seem winded. "No," I lied. My legs felt like they were going to buckle. I leaned up against the car.

"You didn't hear me?" He had an amused look on his face.

"Well," I started to stumble over my words. "I-I did . . . Sort of . . . I guess. I mean. I did." I swallowed hard. "But I didn't know who you were . . ."

Yeah, I'll go with that . . .

"You frightened me," I said with some mustered up bravado.

He reached in his back pocket.

Lord, was he going for handcuffs?

I knew this was it for me.

Get your copy here of a FREE ebook
of *Bed & Breakfast Bedlam*, here:

Amazon
Barnes & Noble
Kobo

For more, visit my website:
www.authorabby.com
Follow me on:
Twitter: twitter.com@AbbyVandiver
Instagrram:
www.instagram.com/abbylvandiver
Facebook:
www.facebook.com/authorabbyl.vandiver

About the Author

WALL STREET JOURNAL, USA TODAY, and internationally best selling author, Abby L. Vandiver, is a hybrid author, being both self and traditionally published. She writes as Abby L. Vandiver/Abby Collette and Cade Bentley. Abby has always enjoyed writing, combining that with her gift for telling stories and love of mystery, she became an author.

Starting in 2013, and prior to 2018, Abby self-published more than twenty books. Her debut novel, In the Beginning and its sequels, Irrefutable Proof and Incarnate are fact mixed with fiction, mystery/sci-fi novels not written as action packed or fast paced, but as "what-if" alternative history stories. After those books were published, Abby switched to writing cozy mysteries, she has four self-published series so far, Logan Dickerson Cozy Mystery, Normal Junction Cozy Mystery, Tiny House Mysteries and ABC

Cozy Mystery Series. In 2017, she contracted with Henery Press for a 3-book deal to pen the series Romaine Wilder Mysteries. After signing with an agent in 2018, she authored two traditionally published cozy mystery series, both pubbed by Penguin Berkley: _An Ice Cream Parlor Mystery's_ and _A Books & Biscuits Mystery_. Switching genres, Abby has penned a women's fiction book, published by Lake Union, _Where Wild Peaches Grow_, due out August 30, 2022, which has received a starred review from Booklist. Abby acted as agent and editor for an anthology comprised of twenty authors of color titled, _Midnight Hour_ published by Crooked Lane.

Although she writes mostly mystery, Abby has co-written a historical/women's fiction novel with author and friend, Kathryn Dionne under the pen name Kathryn Longino, and a Kindle World, historical/sci-fi fiction book, Countdown to Atlantis. That book was inspired by the A.G. Riddle's book, The Atlantis Gene.

During her non-writing life, Abby obtained a bachelors in Economics, a masters in Public Administration and a Juris Doctorate. She is a former attorney and Economics professor, but now writes books full-time for the past nine years. As part of her writing journey, Abby teaches writing classes at her local library, with Literary Cleveland and the International Women's Writing Guild. She will be the Writer in Residence at the South Euclid-Lyndhurst Public Library's William N. Skirball Writer's Center for 2022-2023.

Abby resides in South Euclid, Ohio and enjoys spending time with her grandchildren, all of whom are her favorite.

Romaine Wilder Mystery Series
Secrets, Lies & Crawfish Pies
Love, Hope, & Marriage Tropes
Potions, Spells, & Deadly Tells

An Ice Cream Parlor Mystery Series
A Deadly Inside Scoop
A Game of Cones
A Killer Sunday

Books & Biscuits Mystery Series
Body and Soul Food
Soul of a Killer

Standalones
Where Wild Peaches Grow

Short Stories & Anthologies
Midnight Hour
Murder About Town
Faking the President
A Christmas Present
Baby It's Cold Outside